"Who said ours would be a loveless marriage?" Lilly asked

When Finn said nothing, she continued. "The past few days you've shown me in a hundred tiny ways what kind of man you are. I love the way you buy ice cream for the neighbors' kids. I love how you cared for me when I was sick. You're constantly caring for everyone around you, Finn Reilly, but never for yourself. Well, you know what?"

"What?"

"It's about time someone started caring for you. And I nominate…me." Lilly kissed him. Softly at first, testing. But then he groaned. Leaning back, he pulled her on top of him.

Finn sighed. "I know this may sound crazy, but knowing you're one hundred percent committed to our marriage does amazing things to me."

"Oh, Finn…" *Tell him about the baby,* Lilly's conscience urged. *Before it's too late.*

Dear Reader,

Welcome to Harlequin American Romance, where you're guaranteed heartwarming, emotional and deeply romantic stories set in the backyards, big cities and wide-open spaces of America. Kick starting the month is Cathy Gillen Thacker's *Her Bachelor Challenge*, which launches her brand-new family-connected miniseries THE DEVERAUX LEGACY. In this wonderful story, a night of passion between old acquaintances has a sought-after playboy businessman questioning his bachelor status.

Next, Mollie Molay premieres her new GROOMS IN UNIFORM miniseries. In *The Duchess & Her Bodyguard*, protecting a royal beauty was easy for a by-the-book bodyguard, but falling in love wasn't part of the plan! Don't miss *Husbands, Husbands…Everywhere!* by Sharon Swan, in which a lovely B & B owner's ex-husband shows up on her doorstep with amnesia, giving her the chance to rediscover the man he'd once been. This poignant reunion romance story is the latest installment in the WELCOME TO HARMONY miniseries. Laura Marie Altom makes her Harlequin American Romance debut with *Blind Luck Bride*, which pairs a jilted groom with a pregnant heroine in a marriage meant to satisfy the terms of a bet.

This month, and every month, come home to Harlequin American Romance—and enjoy!

Best,

Melissa Jeglinski
Associate Senior Editor
Harlequin American Romance

BLIND LUCK BRIDE
Laura Marie Altom

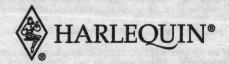

TORONTO • NEW YORK • LONDON
AMSTERDAM • PARIS • SYDNEY • HAMBURG
STOCKHOLM • ATHENS • TOKYO • MILAN • MADRID
PRAGUE • WARSAW • BUDAPEST • AUCKLAND

For Margaret Daley, Mary Jane Morgan,
Cathy Morgan, Judy Pelfrey and Ada Sumner—
the best plot doctors and friends a girl could ever have.
Oh, and thanks for helping out with that demonic hero thing, too!

For Crystal Stovall, Karen Crane and Genell Dellin—
thanks for the breakfasts, lunches and hugs!

And finally, for Lilly, the wriggling, licking, gnawing dachshund princess of
the Alisch family. This book is especially for you, sweetie, because like the
heroine in this book you're constantly finding trouble, but you're so cute
we let you get away with it…most of the time.

ISBN 0-373-16940-X

BLIND LUCK BRIDE

Copyright © 2002 by Laura Marie Altom.

ABOUT THE AUTHOR

After college (Go Hogs!), Laura Marie Altom did a brief stint as an interior designer before becoming a stay-at-home mom to boy/girl twins. Always an avid romance reader, Laura knew it was time to try her hand at writing when she found herself replotting the afternoon soaps. She has written three romances for another publisher. This is her first Harlequin American Romance novel.

When not writing, Laura enjoys a glamorous lifestyle of lounging by a pool that's always in need of cleaning, zipping around in a convertible while trying to keep her dog from leaping out, and is constantly striving to reach the bottom of the laundry basket—a feat she may never accomplish! For real fun, Laura is content to read, do needlepoint and cuddle with her handsome hubby.

Laura loves hearing from readers at either P.O. Box 2074, Tulsa, OK 74101, or e-mail: BaliPalm@aol.com.

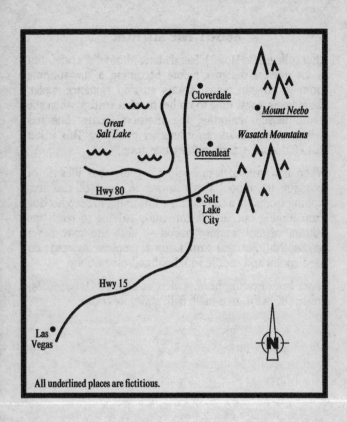

Cloverdale

Mount Neebo

Great
Salt Lake

Wasatch Mountains

Greenleaf

Hwy 80

Salt
Lake
City

Hwy 15

Las
Vegas

N

All underlined places are fictitious.

Chapter One

"Mitch, you're just as dumb as you look. Why, I could find another bride just like that." Before taking another swig of his long-neck beer, Finn Reilly snapped his fingers to emphasize just how easy the task would be.

Good Lord, hadn't he already been through enough today by being jilted at the altar? So why was Mitch Mulligan, his biggest contracting competitor and pain in his neck still giving him grief? Maybe if he closed his eyes, the three-hundred-pound genetic throwback to the woolly mammoth would vanish. Just in case, Finn blinked.

Damn, his bad luck hadn't changed.

"Oh yeah?" Mitch said—and his beer breath—in Finn's face. "Well, I'm gettin' sick and tired of you thinkin' you're so hot with the women 'round here, Reilly."

"That's 'cause you're jealous."

"Ha! Jealous of what? The way your pretty little filly practically *galloped* out of that church to get away from you?"

Finn rolled his beer bottle across his throbbing forehead. Why did everyone keep bringing up the speed with which Vivian had left the church? While she'd vroomed into the sunset with that leather-wearing, motorcycle-riding bandit she met at the Department of Motor Vehicles, Finn had stood abandoned at the altar. Now honestly, did it seem as if he'd been at fault for their troubles?

Why couldn't everyone at Lu's Bar remember he was the injured party?

"Well, Reilly?" Mitch said. "What've you got to say for yourself?"

"Look, Mulligan." Matt Marshall, Finn's best friend since junior high, hollered above the dart-throwing, off duty firemen. "Give the guy a break. Can't you see he's in pain?"

"Pain? *Pain?*" Mitch laughed so hard he spouted beer all over the bar. "Oh, now that's ripe. I always knew you were the prissy type, Reilly, but Matt here just gave me proof."

"Can it," Matt said. "My bud, Reilly, is no more prissy than your mother."

"What'd you say about my mother?" Despite his size, Mitch scrambled to his feet in two-point-five seconds. "Nobody insults my mother without—"

A loud whistle came from behind the bar.

Finn winced.

Crazy Lu and her settle-down-boys banshee blast were landmarks in the small town of Greenleaf, Utah. She'd owned the burger and beer joint for as long as anyone could remember and while she put up with a lot of things, fights weren't one of them. "Mitch Mulligan, either take it outside or take it up with me."

White-haired Lu couldn't have topped five feet wearing heels and a tiara, but the row of ornery guys standing at the bar backed down as if their own mothers had issued the command.

Everyone, that is, except for the woolly mammoth. "Oh now, Lu, don't go gettin' your panties in a wad."

"How do you even know I wear panties, Mitch? I agree with Matt. Just this once, give Reilly a break. Here," she shoved a paper plate heaped with orange-rose-laden wedding cake across the bar. "Put some food in your belly. It'll make you feel better. You prob'ly got gas from all that beer. It's makin' you nasty as a three-headed rattler."

"I don't want any cake and I'm always this nasty. The only thing I want a piece of is that punk sittin' over there shaking in his boots."

"Fine." She winked Finn's way. "Then make him a good honest bet. Just don't mess up his pretty face for the next girl in line for his kisses."

"Why, thank you, sweetheart." Finn winked boldly. At least someone loved him, even if it wasn't the stacked redhead he'd *planned* to be loving right about now.

"Sure thing, angel."

Mitch snorted. "Angel, my—"

"Watch it," Lu warned.

"Ha. All I wanna *watch* is how much crow Reilly here eats when he loses this bet." Mitch pulled a wad of cash from the front pocket of his dingy jeans, peeled off ten hundred-dollar bills, then smacked them on the bar. "All right, pretty boy. I've got a thousand bucks—my entire payroll—says there's no way you can find another woman stupid enough to marry you by the end of the week.''

''Mulligan,'' Lu warned. ''There's families depending on that pay. Don't go bettin' away their suppers.''

With a wave of one of the massive paws he called hands, he brushed her off. ''This here's a sure bet. No one's gonna lose but ol' Reilly here. And seein' how he just got the contract on that fancy new highway motel, he's got plenty of cash to spare.''

Finn rolled his eyes. Was Mulligan ever going to get over the fact that Finn's Custom Building consistently got more jobs than AAA Construction?

''Whatsa matter, pretty boy? Too chicken to take me up on a bet you know you're gonna lose?''

That's it. Finn slammed his bottle on the bar, then grappled to his feet.

Nobody called him prissy, pretty boy *and* chicken all on the same night—especially not when his own aunt had called him a *poor, sweet thing* just that afternoon. ''By God, Mulligan, I'll not only take you up on that bet—'' he pulled honeymoon cash from the chest pocket of his tux, counting out a grand before smacking it beside Mitch's ''—but I'll raise the stakes by throwing in my truck.''

''Finn,'' Lu said. ''You're a bright boy. Be sensible. This is marriage we're talkin' about. A lifetime commitment—not to mention a brand spankin' new black Chevy.''

''All respects, ma'am, but stay out of it—and I'm far from a *boy*.'' He took another swig of beer. ''I'm Grade A, genuine, *M-A-N*. And if it takes a stupid bet to prove any woman would be thrilled to marry me, then by God, bettin' is what I'll do.'' He shoved the pile of money toward Lu. ''Sweetheart, hold on to this until next Saturday night. If I'm not back wearin' a ring by then…well, then you'd better give all that cash to old ugly over there.'' He gestured to Mitch. ''He'll be needin' it to pay for my funeral, 'cause one thing's for sure…''

''What's that?''

''If I'm not married by Saturday, I must be stone-cold dead.''

''No, NO, NO,'' Lilly Churchill cried, stomping her white satin pumps in frustration. Unfortunately, all that fussing raised a dust cloud, which caused her to sneeze, which in turn caused her to need a tissue—a tissue that was in her purse.

On the front seat.

Snuggled alongside her keys.

Keys to the car she'd just securely locked.

''Not now,'' she said to an audience of a million twinkling stars. ''Not when I was for once getting things right.'' Hot tears threatened to spill, but she stoically held them back. This was not the time for a crying binge.

Hiking her heavy white skirts, she teetered across the restaurant's gravel lot.

So, on the eve of her wedding she'd locked her keys in the car? Big deal.

It wasn't an omen that her marriage was doomed. After all, look what'd happened at her big sister Mary's wedding, and four years later, her marriage was still going strong.

Yeah, her conscience butted in, *but don't forget you were the cause of Mary and her three bridesmaids arriving over two hours late for her ceremony.*

And how Robby the groom freaked out because he thought Mary had cold feet. And speaking of cold— remember how the delay caused the reception caterers to run out of Sterno to heat their hot wings, mini-pizzas, and quiches? Ick. To this day, Lilly could still taste the congealed grease.

Her brothers—and even Mary—assured their *baby* sister that running out of gas on the way to the ceremony hadn't been her fault. That the old Nova's gas gauge had always been cranky—especially below an eighth of a tank. But no matter how many times Lilly told herself the mishap could have happened to anyone, she knew that simply wasn't true.

How? From the disappointment in her mom and dad's eyes. From the looks that said how could such a rotten apple have landed in their perfect bushel?

The truth of the matter was that her sister's wedding wasn't the first time Lilly had seen those looks. They'd been there when she dropped out of the University of Utah after her first semester. They'd been there every time she'd lost her retainer, left the milk out, forgotten to take out the trash or feed the dog, bombed a high school final, missed curfew or lost a job. The list went on and on.

For Lilly's whole life, her older, overachieving, straight-A brothers and sisters had done their best to cover up for her when she failed. They'd treated her like a pet they hated to see punished, but now that all of them were busy leading fabulous careers and marriages, she felt lost and alone in trying to figure out what she wanted to do with her life. She thought she knew, but then this whole mess had happened with Elliot, and now…

Now all she wanted to do was make her troubles go away—a goal easily enough accomplished by marrying Dallas. But then what? Would her parents view her marriage as just another bandage? Or, as for the first time in her twenty-five years, her way of taking responsibility for her biggest ever blunder?

FINN CRADLED his forehead in his hands.

Ugh, had he truly drunk all six of the long-necks standing like a row of not-so-pretty maidens on the bar?

The queasy churning in his gut, not to mention the sour taste on his tongue, told him that, yes, not only had he downed all those beers, but he'd downed them in a hurry.

What was the matter with him? He knew better than to drink like that—especially over a woman, but darn it all, he was ready to settle down. Seemed like he'd been ready ever since his parents and sister died when he was eight.

This afternoon he'd been damned close to making his dream of starting over with a new family finally come true, but then Vivian had pulled her disappearing act. Not only had she ruined their wedding by walking out right in the middle of it, but she'd stolen their honeymoon tickets to Cancun.

At the very least, he and Matt could have been

toasting Finn's sorrows beachside instead of in this stinkin' bar.

He raised his head to look around.

For eleven o'clock on Halloween night, the crowd had grown thin. Old Judge Crawford sat in his usual booth in the corner, and Betty and Bob Bristow, the county's finest line dancers, two-stepped to a honky-tonk tune blaring from the jukebox. They made a cute couple in their alien costumes. Doc Walsh and her house husband wore hospital whites—Mr. Walsh wearing a not-too-flattering nurse's cap and gown.

Though not a single patron currently held a cigarette, a thick haze clung to the renovated barn's ceiling, accompanied by the smell of one too many grease fires.

Finn shook his head.

Yep, after today, he was supposed to have been living the good life. Eating plenty of home-cooked meals. Getting back rubs. Indulging in stimulating conversation and—

What the…

A woman—no, an angel—stood at the red vinyl door. Dressed in a gown of gossamer-white, carrying a bouquet of full pink roses, she looked ready to star in a wedding.

Even worse—or maybe better—she was headed his way.

"Excuse me?" she asked, her melodic voice about as loud as a marshmallow being dropped on a cloud. "But…are you by any chance…"

"Waiting to get married?" This had to be a joke. Mulligan had to have sent her.

"Yes, me too. I'm Lilly and you must be Dallas."
Dallas?

She held out her hand. A tiny, white-gloved affair that when he briefly gripped it, felt lost in Finn's palm. *Lilly.* Such a fitting name for this delicate flower of a woman.

A rush of protectiveness flooded his system.

But wait a minute... Since Mitch had obviously hired this woman to mess with Finn's head, why should he feel anything for her, let alone protective?

Giving the blonde a cool appraisal, in his mind's eye, Finn unfurled the enemy's master plan. Mitch must have met this "bride" at a buddy's Halloween party, then bribed her to feign interest in Finn. Hell, maybe he'd even paid her enough to pretend she was actually going to marry him, then, just when Finn wagged a marriage license in the mammoth's ugly face, Mitch would drop his bomb that this angel was no bride, but someone he hired to cause Finn to lose the bet! To most folks' way of thinking, Finn would have won by marrying, but Mitch wasn't most folks. Mitch was crafty—wily enough to deduce that if Finn wed a bride who was lying about her name, then the marriage wouldn't be legal. Thus causing Finn to lose on a technicality.

And trust Mitch to have not even thought his plan through well enough to tell the woman the name of the guy she was supposed to dupe. "Yep," Finn said with a knowing smile. "I'm Dallas. That's me."

"Thank goodness. I've been driving for hours. I never thought I'd find this place." Her shoulders sagged. "Even now, Dallas, I must say I'm surprised.

When you described *Luigi's,* I thought it would be a little more…"

Finn followed her sweeping, and maybe even a bit fearful, gaze as it flitted from face to face to land on old drunken Pete who sat half-asleep and mumbling at the other end of the bar.

"You thought *this* was Luigi's?" That place was the swankiest restaurant for miles. Swallowing hard, Finn blocked the memory of how beautiful Vivian had looked the night he'd taken her there to propose.

"Well…yes. It is, isn't it? I saw the *L-U*-apostrophe-*S* on the sign."

"Sure. This is *Lu*-igi's. I'm glad you found it."

"Me, too." She licked her lips. Kissable lips. Lips that on a good night could drive a man all the way to distraction.

After the day he'd had, did he feel like going for a ride? *Hell, yes.*

"So?" she said. "Shouldn't we get going? I made all the plans. All we have to do is…exchange our vows." She smoothed the front of her satin gown, looking up at him with impossibly wide, impossibly blue eyes.

He gulped.

Mitch had certainly done his homework in hiring this gal. She was a real pro to have almost had Finn falling for her—*almost.*

"I was afraid you wouldn't come," Lilly said, fighting the urge to flee. When Dallas had said in that morning's e-mail that he was suit-and-tie handsome, he'd been way off in his description. Deliciously off.

She couldn't *really* marry a man like him, could she?

Do I really *have a choice?* It wasn't as if guys were lined up around the block waiting to marry a woman in her condition.

"Not come?" He snatched a French fry from a basket on the bar. She tracked his hand all the way to his mouth. A mouth with lips that looked chiseled from the most fascinating stone. "How could I have stayed away from our big day? Or—" another fry in hand, he waved toward a darkened window "—I guess that would be night."

When he spied her gaze lingering on his mouth, he offered her his latest fry, but she shook her head, flushed with heat at the mere possibility of consuming food that had come so perilously close to his lips.

She cleared her throat. "I, ah, don't blame you if you've changed your mind. I mean, this is kind of sudden."

"Nonsense." He swallowed his bite of fry.

"It's okay. Really. I wouldn't be too upset if you want to back out."

"Nope. Not me."

"Great." Lilly released the breath she hadn't realized she'd been holding. In the month they'd known each other via the Marriage of Convenience board on Singles.com, this was what she liked more every day about Dallas. He was a man driven by convictions. Okay, so he wasn't marrying her out of love, but his conviction to succeed in his ultraconservative law firm—the same firm that told him he needed a wife—

but she was okay with that. All she needed was a husband—the rest would work itself out in time.

"Let's go," she said. "I set up the ceremony for ten tomorrow morning, but even driving all night, that doesn't give us much time."

"All night? I don't get it."

"Vegas. That's where we'll be taking our vows. Remember? How you told me your mother always wanted to be married there?"

"Oh." He conked his temple. "Of course. *Mom. The Elvis Chapel.* How could I forget?"

"I thought she liked Wayne Newton?"

"Um… Wayne, Elvis, she liked 'em all."

Lilly drew her lower lip into her mouth and nibbled. As relieved as she'd been only a minute earlier to have finally found her man, something now told her riding off into the night with this virtual stranger wasn't one of her brighter ideas. It didn't matter that she and Dallas had talked via e-mail for the better part of a month. His not remembering his own mother's favorite recording artist concerned her. Where was the man who bragged of having a photographic memory? The man who cited countless statistics on the reasons why arranged marriages were infinitely better than the real thing?

The whisker-stubbled, bona fide stud seated before her surely didn't give a flip about dry statistics, and he looked as if he'd be far more comfortable listening to a Garth Brooks song than to *Aida*, his supposedly favorite opera.

Should she ask to see his driver's license?

No. Too direct. Yes, she needed to verify he was

who he said he was, but surely she could think of a less combatant way. She cleared her throat. "I, ah, realize this may sound a tad off the subject, but could you please tell me what my favorite food is?"

His eyes narrowed, and he took a long time before saying in a sexy twang, "Aw, now, *angel,* you already know that I know what your favorite food is." He reached for her left hand and rolled down the cuff of her satin glove, exposing the frantically beating pulse on her inner wrist. "Why don't you ask me something a little tougher...."

Oh my gosh! He was actually drawing her wrist to his mouth! He was—oh no. Oh no, he did not just kiss her on the wrist. As an employee of Tree House Books, she read a lot, but in her favorite novel of all time, *Whispered Winds,* the hero, Duncan, kissed his bride's wrist at their third wedding. True, it had taken them three times to get their relationship right, but oh, how right it had finally been. Favorite food be damned. The fact that Dallas remembered how much she adored that scene proved beyond a shadow of a doubt that he was not only who he claimed to be, but that first and foremost, he was the man destined to be her husband.

Closing her eyes, Lilly surrendered to the hot-cold champagne bubbles zinging through her body.

The white-haired woman keeping bar interrupted Lilly's almost-wedded bliss. "S'cuse me," she said to Dallas, "but what in tarnation do you think you're doin'?"

"Mind your own business, Lu, this is my future bride."

"Isn't one bride per day enough for you, Fi—"

"That's it. We've gotta go." Finn nearly fell off his bar stool trying to slip his hand beneath his bride-to-be's elbow while at the same time shooting Lu a would-you-please-hush look of desperation. By God, if she went and ruined this for him, he'd take her to court to cover the small fortune in cash and pride he'd have to fork over to Mitch. He might be able to handle a lot of bad situations, but voluntarily losing a bet to ornery old Mitch Mulligan wasn't one of them. He knew it wasn't neighborly, but he just plain despised the man, and he'd do anything to get the better of him. Even if it meant marrying this loco filly in the morning only to up and divorce her the next afternoon.

While all that sounded real good in theory, a pang of confusion rippled through Finn at the all-too-fresh memory of how badly Vivian had hurt him.

All his life he'd only wanted one thing—to once again be part of a family. So sure, by going through with this marriage, he'd make Mitch look like the fool he was, but in doing that, he'd also be making a mockery of his heart's lifelong ambition. Was that wise?

A whiff of pretty-as-a-spring-meadow perfume wove its way like a love potion through Finn's senses. He took one look at the vision in bridal white standing before him and decided what the heck?

He needed to lighten up.

Besides, what was the worst that could happen on a trip to Vegas?

Chapter Two

"Ready, darlin'?" Finn said, low enough so that hope-fully Lu wouldn't hear.

"I sure am." Lilly waved to the still-gaping older woman. "Bye-bye."

Lu might have been willing to let the whole incident slide if only Finn's bride hadn't—from out of no-where—burst into tears.

"Now, now," Lu crooned, zipping around the cor-ner of the bar. "What's the matter?"

"I—I'm so ha-ha-happy," Lilly blurted in the same kind of hormonal, nonsensical, downright blithering sobs that had taken over Matt's sister the day after she found out she was pregnant. "But I've waited so long for my wedding day, and Dallas, you're even more of a gentleman than I'd imagined, but...I just remem-bered I locked my keys in my car, and..."

Lu's eagle eyes bored into Finn's forehead like twin laser beams. After pulling Lilly in close for a hug, she said, "Now, honey, 'round here folks lock themselves out of all sorts of things. Don't you worry. Your *groom* knows just what to do."

Never had Finn wished harder that he lived in a less nosy town.

After a few more minutes of what Finn considered award-winning acting, Lilly calmed down, her smile shining brighter than the chrome on Vivian's boyfriend's motorcycle. "I'm sorry," she said. "I don't kn-know what came over me, especially when you had such great news about the keys."

"Emotions'll do that to a body," Lu said, lapping up this rare opportunity to cluck over one of her patrons. "How about you visit the little girl's room. Freshen up while your, ah, groom gets started on your car—if he's sober enough."

"That'd be great," Lilly said through a watery smile. She looked Finn's way. "You don't mind the short delay, do you?"

Mind? Hell, yes, he minded. Not only didn't he like the idea of spending the next hour or so outside with a coat hanger and flashlight, but once he got this human tear-bucket into her car, did that imply driving it and her all the way to Vegas? It was on the tip of his tongue to call off this whole charade when he caught sight of those wide-open skies his bride called eyes. Never had he seen eyes more blue. On manly autopilot, he said, "Ah, sure, I don't mind. You go on and do whatever you need to and I'll just be outside."

"You remember what I drive?" she asked, her voice all breathy, as if his knowing such a fact guaranteed theirs would be a lifelong love.

"Sure, darlin'." *Simple logic tells me it'll be the only spit-shined sedan in the lot.*

More to prove to Lu that he had the woman's best

interests at heart than to satisfy his own blazing curiosity as to the feel of her petal-soft lips, he slipped his free hand about Lilly's waist and kissed her hard—not too hard—just hard enough to let her know she was in the company of a real man. Mitch Mulligan might be signing her paycheck, but Finn Reilly was calling the shots.

When she seemed good and dazed by his prowess, with a quick pat to her satin-covered behind, he sent her in the direction of the ladies' room.

But just as he was growing accustomed to the sight of his bride-to-be's backside, Lu grabbed him by the ear and yanked for all she was worth—not an easy feat considering he was well over a foot taller than she. "You low-life, back-stabbin', pitiful excuse for a yellow-bellied—"

"Ouch!" he complained, backing out of her reach. "That hurts."

"Damn straight, it hurts. Almost as much as that alley cat Vivian hurt you this afternoon. Don't you see what you're doin'?"

"What do you mean?"

"You know exactly what I mean. Look, son, and make no mistake, over the years you've been comin' in here, I've grown to think of you as my own son. What you could end up doin' to this girl is the same thing Vivian did to you. You're gonna lead her on, then dump her. Only at least Vivian dumped you for love. You, on the other hand, will be freein' yourself up for a truck named Abigail."

"Slow down, Lu, you don't know the half of what's going on." Challenging her steely gaze with one of his own, he said, "Shoot, Mitch put my *bride* up to this. That woman's no innocent. I mean, come on, unless she was being paid darned good money, what would a gal like her be doing in a place like this? No offense."

"None taken, but, Finn," she said, sounding all too much like the aunt who had raised him—the same aunt who had been living in Miami, blessedly out of scolding distance, for going on five years. "I don't know who this girl is, but one thing I do know just from lookin' at her is that she's not messed up with Mitch. Maybe she has amnesia or somethin'? All I'm sayin' is be careful."

"Lu, like you said, you know me. I'm not planning to hurt anyone."

"No, I'm sure you're not, but you be careful anyway, 'cause now that I think about it, the only one gettin' hurt around here might be you."

"Ready?" asked the angel in white.

"Yeah, I'm—" Finn looked up, only to have his heart lurch at the sight of her. He'd always fancied himself as preferring redheads, but this blond-haired beauty had brushed her curls into an adorable halo that looped and swirled about the heart-shaped contours of her face. She'd applied a light coat of lipstick that accentuated the faint swelling caused by his kiss. Whew, Mitch sure had improved his taste in women! "I'm ready," he said. "Sorry I didn't get a chance to get the car."

"That's okay. Once you get the keys out, probably with what you've had to drink, it's better that I drive.

We wouldn't want anything to further delay our trip to the chapel, would we?''

No. Hell no.

To Lu, his angel said, "Ma'am, it was sure nice meeting you, and thank you for—" she held up a wadded pink tissue "—for helping me see that Dallas is the only man for me."

Upon hearing another man's name in association with Finn, Lu's eyebrows shot up like a pair of jackrabbits scared out of their holes. She looked to him, then the woman in white. "You're welcome, child. And the only thanks I need is the promise you two will share a *lifetime* worth of happiness."

That did it.

His bride's waterworks started all over again, but this time, she turned to Finn for her hugs. Never had he felt more masculine than holding this petite thing in his arms. Never had he felt more in control. This gal was a mighty fine actress, but no one fooled Finn Reilly. He could smell one of Mitch's tricks from a mile away.

Once she broke her hug, Finn slipped his arm around her slight waist and led her out of the bar as fast as his black dress boots could scoot.

Outside, feet firmly planted on the pea gravel driveway, his gaze aimed at the stars, Finn gulped gallons of the crisp fall air. Had there ever been a luckier man than he? Yep, having Mitch arrange for this fallen angel to enter his life was just about the best damned shot of blind luck he'd ever had. Winning this bet was not only going to be easy, but a ton of fun.

Confirming that thought, his bride snuggled close,

resting her head on his chest. Her soft curls tickled the bottom of his chin. He'd always liked it when a woman fit him—even a woman he was only pretending to like.

He and Vivian had stood eye to eye. She'd been a bad fit.

"Dallas?" Lilly said.

"Yeah?"

"I just want you to know, before tomorrow, that I really appreciate you doing this for me. And…and one day, I hope we'll not just share a marriage license, but maybe even a special friendship."

A special friendship? Ugh.

Time to raise the stakes.

"Dallas?"

Not thinking, just doing, Finn cinched her closer, planting his lips atop hers for a powerful kiss.

"Mmm, Dallas," she said on a sigh that was more of a purr.

She started kissing him back, but the voltage of their second embrace caught Finn off guard and he pulled away.

Nope.

No way had he enjoyed that marathon smooch to the degree his racing heart implied.

To prove he was still in complete control of not only the situation, but his feelings, he kissed his bride-to-be all over again. When she mewed her pleasure, he fought to hold back a moan. Lord, they were good together.

Had he and Vivian ever been like this? Maybe once, or maybe he'd only wished they could be. Damn, what was happening to him? He knew better than to be sucked into the spell of another conniving woman.

"Mmm, Dallas." She pulled away with a whispery sigh. "I didn't know that outside of the movies a kiss could be that good."

They usually weren't. "Yeah…well, what can I say?"

She smiled and the heartbreaking beauty of it nearly stole the breath from his lungs. "I know what I'd like you to say."

"What's that?"

"Ask me to marry you. I've read it in your letters, but I've never heard you say it. Say it, Dallas. *Please.*" As strong as Lilly had felt only moments earlier, Dallas's kiss had left her that weak. Her knees felt rubbery and her chest strangely tight with anticipation and tingling warmth. Was a marriage of convenience supposed to be this much fun?

"How can I ask you to marry me when I don't know your name?"

"Excuse me?"

"You know, your, ah, *full* name."

Thank goodness. *Her full name.* Of course. She'd almost been back to her original worry that maybe this man wasn't Dallas after all. "My given name is Lillian Diane Churchill. But, please, feel free to keep on calling me Lilly. There's no need for you to get formal on me now."

"Okay, *Lilly*…" He paused after drawling the *l*'s. Never before had just hearing her name brought such heady pleasure. "Will you marry me?"

Would she marry him? She'd follow him to the end

of the earth and back—that is, assuming he never lied to her. Elliot had lied, and look what she'd gotten from him. That's why she knew things were going to work out great with Dallas. Their relationship was based upon total honesty.

She licked her lips, took a deep breath and committed every second of this moment to memory. She'd remember the way Dallas smelled, like…well, a little like beer and cigarette smoke, but beneath all that, she detected citrus aftershave and a distinctly delicious scent that was all him—and soon to be all hers! "Yes, Dallas. Of course, I'll marry you."

"Good. Then how about you and me getting this show on the road?"

"Mr. Lebeaux, it would be my pleasure."

"Who's *Mr. Lebeaux?*"

"Oh, Dallas," she said, her giddy laugh carrying across the still night air. "You're so funny."

Not so funny, though, was when, a few minutes later, Dallas calmly opened her car's passenger door to reach for her keys. How could she have been so scatterbrained as to not even check the other door to see if it was unlocked?

"This is embarrassing," she mumbled. She would have added that since finding out about the baby, she hadn't been feeling herself, but the problem was that incidents like this were exactly herself. Good grief, she was soon going to be a mother. She had to start being more responsible.

"There you go," Finn said. Wearing a bemused grin, he handed her a wad of interconnected souvenir key chains. "Guess we'll chalk this incident up to bridal jitters."

"I'm afraid it's more than that," she said, placing her hand protectively over her tummy.

"Oh? Confession time?"

"Only on the matter that you're about to wed a misfit. I thought our marriage would instantly transform me, but so far, I guess it hasn't worked."

"We're not hitched yet," he pointed out. "Maybe saying those all-important vows is all you need to turn your life around?"

"You think?" She looked at him, *really* looked at the man she would spend the next fifty years with. And what she saw wasn't just a handsome face and warm, expressive brown eyes, but for the first time in the month they'd corresponded, she saw that perhaps instead of this marriage being the platonic business arrangement she'd expected, there just might be a chance of something more.

THE NEXT MORNING, after finally pulling into the chapel parking lot for some shut-eye, Finn woke to a delicious weight resting on his chest. From his perch behind the wheel—somewhere around one in the morning he'd taken over the driving—he saw a crown of silken gold contrasting with the black wool of his tux. To test if his latest fiancée was real, he looped his finger around one of her baby-fine curls. She shifted and moaned, granting him a breathtaking view of her profile.

Yep, she was real all right. A real knockout.

Let the games continue!

Warm sun beat through the car windows, illuminating honeyed highlights in her eyebrows and lashes. Her lips looked every bit as plump and kissable as they had the night before, and the brief memory of the way that mouth had felt touching his caused a swelling down south that made his pants even more uncomfortable.

As his future bride again stirred against him, spilling the softest of mews, Finn wondered what the hell he was doing? The marriage license they'd obtained near dawn rested heavy in his chest pocket, as did the fact that he'd had to slip the clerk a hundred while Lilly had been in the courthouse bathroom to fill out the document in his real name.

During the night's long drive, while Lilly softly snored, he'd reconfirmed his belief that her calling him *Dallas* had to be part of Mitch's grand scheme. For if Finn were to marry Lilly using a false name—to insure that she didn't know he was on to her plan—their marriage wouldn't be legal, thus giving Mitch the right to drive off in Abigail on a technicality. But as usual, Finn was one step ahead of his nemesis.

The one thing Finn hadn't counted on was being this attracted to his bride. Still, he supposed his attraction to her would add a certain touch of realism to their ceremony—even if it was just pretend.

"Lilly," he said, deciding the time had come to guarantee his winning the bet. "Hello? Are you ready to tie the knot?"

"Hmm?"

"Hello? Wake up." He softly tickled behind her

right ear. "We're at the Wayne Newton Chapel, just like you requested."

She took a second to wake, then eased upright, quickly processing the fact that she'd been using his chest as a pillow. "Sorry," she said, unaware of the adorable red mark on the left side of her face from where she'd pressed her cheek against his lapel.

"How do you feel?" she asked, scooting to her half of the front seat. From the dashboard, she reached for her bouquet, which had wilted during the night. The heavy scent of fading pink roses filled the air.

"Feel?" Even as he said the word, his head pounded. "Oh right. *Feel.*" He flashed her a wry grin, hoping his beer breath didn't smell as bad as it tasted. "Actually, not so hot."

"You don't make a habit of drinking that much, do you?"

He shook his head. "Must have been all the excitement."

"Sure. I understand." Pulling down the visor, she gazed into a small lighted mirror and pursed her lips into a frown. "Ugh, looks like that drive took even longer than I thought." She reached to the floorboard for her purse and dove inside, pulling out a tube of lipstick. After giving her lips a pretty sheen, she eyed him funny. "Are you sure you feel up to this?"

"What kind of question is that? You trying to back out on me?"

If he could have bottled the feeling her grin gave him, he'd be a rich man. Gone was his headache and, oddly enough, all his doubts about the vows he was about to take. How the marriage ended they could figure out later. Right now, he planned to enjoy the moment, starting with appreciating his lovely bride.

Her lipstick was the sheerest of pink and, just as she had at Lu's the night before, she did a fluff-and-tuck routine on her hair that left it a tousled, yet somehow elegant, shoulder-length mess. She capped it with her veil, mesmerizing him with the sight of filmy white lace whispering to flushed cheeks. What was she thinking? Did she find herself in the similarly bizarre situation of being as attracted to him as he was to her?

She lifted her hand to his cheek. Here it came, she was about to tell him how hot she was for him....

"You've, um, got something on your face." His heart plummeted when she brushed at a spot to the left of his nose, then held up a gray lint ball for his inspection. "See? I didn't want you wearing this in our wedding photos."

"Right. Ah, me neither." Damn. Could he have possibly misread that situation more completely? This temptress was so sly that for a second she'd *almost* made him forget why they were there.

Trying to hide his consternation with both himself and his bride, he fumed out the dusty car window. At dawn, he'd parked the vehicle in an alley they shared with a primer-gray Impala up on blocks and two overfilled Dumpsters. What were the odds that he'd smell motorcycle exhaust at his first wedding, then week-old trash at his second? "So," he said, rubbing his palms together. "Should we do this thing?"

"You're sure?"

"Why do I keep getting the feeling you're not?"

Lilly returned her attention to her purse. "I don't

know…because I don't feel the slightest bit apprehensive." Her digging took on a furious pace. Could she really go through with this? Sure, making her parents proud and all was a very big deal, but after what Elliot had put her through, did she feel ready to open her heart to another man?

Whoa.

She scavenged her purse even faster.

Who'd said anything about doing anything with her heart? This was a marriage of convenience. The love-match line formed on the other side of the building.

"What are you looking for?"

"Mints. I've got to have mints. I don't want to say my vows with bad breath."

Grasping her by the wrists, he stilled her hands, then took them in his. "Lilly, you smell fine, you look beautiful. Trust me, there's nothing for you to be worried about."

"Really? I look okay? I don't look as though I was up all night driving?"

He grinned. "How could you when you've been sleeping on me for the better part of the last—" he eyed his watch "—eight hours. It would have been nine, but remember when we dealt with that pesky business of getting our license?"

"Oh, yeah. I forgot. So I slept all that time?"

"Peaceful as a baby."

Smoothing the front of her gown, she said, "Yes, well…"

Finn's stomach took a dive. *Was* she thinking of backing out? She'd better not. He had a lot at stake. Not only a brand-new truck that wasn't even paid for, but a massive amount of pride. He *had* to win this bet. Still, maybe if she was getting cold feet, he should take it easy on her, act as if he had all the time in the world for them to make their vows. "Maybe we should wait?" he suggested. "We could get a room. You could take a nap and freshen up, then, once you feel up to it, we'll get hitched tonight."

"You want to get a room? Now?" There went those eyes of hers again. Big blue saucers brimming with disapproval.

"Well, sure. Why? What's the matter with our sharing a room?"

"I thought you knew how I felt about such things."

"What things?"

"You know…" She ducked her gaze, aiming it on the yucca plant thriving between Dumpsters number one and two. "Premarital—and in our case, even aftermarital—relations."

"Huh?"

"*S-E-X.*"

"Oh. *Ooh.* Well, who said anything about doing the mattress mambo? All I suggested was that we get a room so you could take a nap."

"That's okay. I'd just as soon get this over with."

Get it over with? What kind of a thing was that for a bride to say? Even a pretend bride! "Ah, sure. Let's go."

He bolted from the car, racing around the now dusty sedan intent on opening her door, but he was too late. She'd already done it. Didn't she know she was being paid to let him do manly stuff for her so that she felt more like a woman and he felt like more of a—

Dope.

While he'd stood there contemplating his manhood, she'd already hustled past the weed-choked side of the pink chapel. Coming around the corner, Finn looked up to see a gigantic statue of smiling Wayne Newton. He held a wedding cake in his hands, and an inscription across the top of the chapel read, *Wayne's House of Love,* and beneath that, *Danke Schoen for your patronage.*

Dear Lord, what am I getting into?

"Lilly! Wait up!" He tried shoving the keys into his pocket, but they wouldn't fit. Her massive key chain was loaded down with a pink rabbit's foot and mini snow-globes from every cheesy destination in the West. "Can you please put this in your purse?"

"Sure," she said, pausing to grab the wad of fuzz and plastic from him, then slip it into her white bag. She glanced at her slim gold watch. "We'd better hurry. We're almost late. Do you have the license?"

"Yeah." *Only it doesn't quite read the way you think it does.* How would she take the news when she learned he'd been on to her scam from the start?

"Hello? Dallas?"

"Huh? Oh—right. I'm ready and rarin' to go."

"No, not yet." She approached him, then, standing on her tiptoes, buttoned his collar and retied his bow tie. The warm brush of her fingers against his throat startled him. Her act was intimate—the kind of thing a wife does for her husband before they attend their daughter's wedding. Again Finn's conscience reminded him of how badly he yearned for that kind of lifelong bliss, and of just how far this sham marriage was from the real thing.

"There," Lilly said with a misty smile. "That's better. Come on, let's get married."

On her way inside, for the umpteenth time Lilly wondered if she was doing the right thing. After all, she was still kind of on the rebound from Elliot, and maybe a month wasn't long enough to know someone before she married him.

Yeah, but on the flip side, she'd known Elliot Dinsmoore all her life. Could she help it if, during the brief time they'd both moved away from their hometown, the charming traveling insurance salesman had gotten married—and conveniently forgot to tell her during their whirlwind romance that he *still was* married?

Shameful heat crept up her cheeks at the memory of the horrific day he'd told her his news. The day she'd given him not only her virginity, but her heart. Even now, almost two months after the fact, she knew that if her perfect family, none of whom had ever done a bad, stupid or reckless thing in their lives, found out she was pregnant with a married man's baby, they'd never forgive her.

Well, she thought, throwing her shoulders back at the same time she opened the mirrored-glass chapel door, this was one time she was doing exactly the right thing. After being dumped by Elliot, she feared she'd never find a father for her baby, but after only a few weeks of online chatting with Dallas, she'd known everything would work out fine.

From her first sight of his out of focus—yet still

cute in a blurry way—online picture, to the way he promised to be a good dad if she promised to be a good hostess, she'd known theirs would be a lasting relationship. A relationship no one ever need know wasn't based on love.

All her adult life, her family had urged her to go to college, to find a *real* job, yet all she could ever remember wanting to do was raise a big brood of kids—just like her own mom. Lilly dreamed of ruling a rambling Victorian home alongside a loving husband, raising not award-winning kids, but rambunctious kids who got into as many jams as she had growing up.

And just think, finally, within a matter of mere minutes, all those dreams would be well on their way to coming true—well, all of them except for the Victorian house and loving husband, but then Lilly glanced over her shoulder just as Dallas stumbled across the threshold from concrete to red-hot-red shag carpet. Even tripping over his own feet, the man was criminally handsome—maybe even more so now that she'd seen he wasn't perfect, either!

He flashed her a smile of strong white teeth, making her tummy flip-flop. Wow. There may never be love in their future, but if he kept that up, at least on her part there was starting to be a disconcerting amount of attraction.

"Hey," he said. "Great taste in chapels."

"You like it?"

"What's not to like?"

Wayne Newton's voice crooned through hidden speakers and pictures of Wayne coated every available inch of wall. A mannequin resplendently dressed in what a plaque at the bottom claimed was a genuine Wayne-worn suit spun in a slow circle. Everything about the place spoke of fun. Las Vegas-style fun. So why did she feel like bursting into tears?

"Hey?" he asked, cupping her face with his big, work-roughened hands. *When had Dallas—an accomplished corporate attorney—ever done a lick of manual labor?* "You look like you're about to spout another eye gusher. Come on, Lil, don't cry."

His mentioning the word *cry* brought on her waterworks. "It's j-just that I…" She gestured to their surroundings, to the dyed blonde, approaching at eleven o'clock who was dressed in head-to-toe black sequins. "Oh, Dallas…" Lilly threw herself at her groom. "I know I told you this was okay, but I always w-wanted to get married in a ch-church." Wishing she wasn't such an emotional basket case, she flashed him an apologetic look, then hefted her skirts in a mad dash for the door marked Powder Room.

"Are we having a problem?" their hostess asked.

Finn shook his head and whispered, "She'll be fine."

"I hope so, because…" Finn followed her gaze to a mirrored grandfather clock that was on chime number four of ten.

"We've got a big group coming in at ten-thirty. Either you two get the show on the road, or I'm afraid we'll have to reschedule you for—"

"No," Finn said, heading for the bathroom door. "No need to reschedule." At least he hoped not! Not only were Lilly's amazingly accurate fake tears tugging at his freshly broken heart, but visions of Mitch driving his truck screamed at his pride. The more Lilly stalled, the more Finn knew Mulligan was paying her to be with him. All this wailing had to be another part of the plan designed to yank his chain. Mitch must have told her to keep an eye on him while letting the bet deadline run out. That way, by the time Finn caught on to the scam, it would be too late to find another—less calculating—bride.

After a few minutes, Finn heard sniffles, then the door creaked open. His adorable, pink-cheeked bride peeked out. "A-after all my b-blubbering," she managed to say, "y-you probably don't want to marry me, do you?" A single tear glistening on her left cheek pierced his conscience.

Good grief, how had this all gotten so complicated?

Suddenly his scheme to win a thousand bucks and make Mitch look bad had somehow taken a back seat to his desire to once again make Lilly smile. "Of course, I want to marry you, sweetheart." *Sweetheart?* "And listen, I was thinking that with this being Sunday morning and all, we could find a church and do this thing right. I mean, our family and friends won't be there, but…"

"Oh, Dallas!" Although her sobs started anew, he spied a smile mixed in with the tears. His feeling of manly pride almost swelled right out of his chest.

Damn, she was good.

While their hostess gaped, Finn figured he might as well prove to her, too, that he was a grade A, genuine, manly *M-A-N*, so he swooped his bride into his arms. Though he could barely see past the tufts of flowery-smelling lace tickling his nose, he ushered Lilly out of the chapel and into brilliant sun.

Chapter Three

An hour later, Lilly beamed when Dallas had not only found her a lofty Methodist church to marry in, but an elderly minister with a few minutes to spare between his first and second services.

Standing in sunbeams shafting through decades-old stained glass, never had Lilly felt more sure about one of her decisions. Rich scents of pale pink cabbage roses and fragile lily of the valley wreathed her senses, bringing her to the conclusion that Dallas Lebeaux was a hero among men.

Not only had he found this church, but at a grocery store he had bought her a glorious new bouquet because he had noticed her old one drooping. Then he'd taken it upon himself to make every moment of their revised ceremony complete, all the way down to wonderfully gaudy, gum-ball machine rings. His TLC calmed her bridal jitters, and for the first time since sealing their arrangement, she didn't feel the slightest bit apprehensive. If anything, she felt oddly excited about the years—and especially, hours—to come.

"Do you, Lillian, take thee Dallas as your lawfully

wedded husband?'' The minister's solemn voice echoed in the lofty space.

"I do,'' she answered strong and clear.

He turned to Dallas. "Do you, Dallas, take thee Lillian to be your lawfully wedded wife?''

"Yeah…I, ah, do.''

"Then by the power vested in me, I hereby pronounce you husband and wife. Dallas, you may kiss your radiant bride.''

As he did just that, Lilly thought she'd melt with bone-deep satisfaction. Her family would be so proud of the way she'd mended the broken pieces of her life—that is, they'd be proud if they knew what kind of mess she'd gotten into. Thankfully, now, they need never know. Her pregnancy cover-up was a fait accompli.

TWENTY-MINUTES LATER, Finn sat behind the wheel of his *wife's* car, driving down a main drag, wondering if taking his marriage vows under another man's name had broken any laws of man, or just God? Telling the kindly, rushed for time, elderly minister he'd left their marriage license all the way back in the car probably hadn't been good, either. But hey, if the minister had noticed the discrepancy in names, Lilly would have been clued in on the fact that her groom was onto her scheme. Finn's stomach churned, but one glance at Lilly did the work of a hundred Rolaids.

Lord, she was a sight to behold.

What was he worried about? He'd already won the bet. Now all he had to do was gloat to Mitch.

Sneaking another peek at his temporary bride, Finn

noticed how her golden curls perfectly matched a magnolia smooth complexion that seemed more suited to Mississippi than the dried-up West. "Have you always lived in Utah?" he asked, stopping the car at a red light.

She eyed him funny. "Are you feeling okay?"

"Sure."

"Then why would you ask me something like that? You know all about my childhood, goofy."

"Right. How could I forget?" Thankfully, the light changed so he could pretend to focus on driving. "Ready to head back to Greenleaf?"

She shot him a look of horror. "Don't you remember?"

"What?"

"Dallas?" Sounding hurt, she said, "I made reservations at the Bridal Fair Theme Motel and Casino. Remember how you said your mother had always wanted to stay there, but hadn't had the money?"

He shook his head. "Aren't you sweet? Here, we've only been married a few minutes and look, already you're taking care of me to the extent that you're worried about my mother." *God rest her soul.*

That brought the roses back to Lilly's cheeks.

Aha! Again, his earlier assumptions had been right. Her wanting them to stay in Vegas was definitely another facet of Mitch's plan. A form of insurance.

Since Lilly thought he had married her under an assumed name, she still believed she'd won the bet for the enemy camp. The only way she wouldn't win was if Finn realized that although he had lost the bet on a technicality, he still had time to find another bride. In short, Lilly had been told to keep her eye on him while letting the clock run down.

Fortunately, Finn was still about twelve steps ahead of her. And given that he'd always loved Vegas and a good party, he figured why not combine those two loves to not only celebrate his victory, but call Lilly's bluff to see just how far she was willing to go for her boss.

"I've got an idea," he said. "How about since my mother isn't here, we stay at one of the big boys? You know, like Luxor or Bally's? Even better, The Venetian—I've heard it's *very* romantic."

She dropped her gaze. Her bottom lip started to quiver. "Y-you said you preferred intimacy over crowds. I mean, though we discussed taking you know—things—slow, I even booked the Mount Vesuvius Suite."

Mmm, smooth move. Looked like she was definitely willing to go all the way, but playing coy.

Eyeing her lips, he remembered how soft they were. Soft and warm and moist and—

"Look out!"

Finn slammed on the breaks, narrowly avoiding a nasty run-in with a diesel-belching city bus.

Instinctively he shot his arm out to brace Lilly should they crash, but with the danger long gone, he gave himself a pat on the back. Way to go, man—not for saving the car, but for accidentally landing a direct hit atop her left breast. Beneath his palm, her nipple swelled and hardened, returning him to high school to watch one of those slow-motion science films on budding flowers. Right before his eyes, or rather his touch, this flower was blooming, and the sight of her flustered smile filled him with awe.

Whew, he thought, taking his sweet time removing his hand. Good thing he had a handle on this situation or he might have mistaken all this lust for genuine attraction.

"Do you need me to drive?" she asked.

"Nope. I've got everything under control." Except for that nagging issue of forgetting he was parked in the middle of a bustling six-lane road.

FIFTEEN MINUTES LATER in a dark, dank-smelling alcove leading to the bathrooms of Elvis's Hunk o' Good Cookin' Café where they'd stopped for brunch, Finn had a hard time transferring the numbers from his calling card to a pay phone. He wasn't trembling, was he? The slight shake to his hands must have been from hunger, because he certainly wasn't that upset about his bothersome fascination with his wife.

Three tries later, the other line rang.

"Yeah?" a groggy Matt finally answered.

"You gotta help me, bud. I'm scared."

"Finn? That you?"

"Yep, and I'm treadin' some pretty deep water."

"What's up?"

"You know that bet I had with Mitch?"

"Uh-huh…"

"Well, to make a long story short, I found a bride and this morning…I married her in Vegas."

"You what?" Instantly Matt's voice went from sleepin'-it-off mode to high-noon alert. "Please tell me you're joking."

"Sorry."

"Oh, man. What're you gonna do? Who is she? Where'd you meet?"

Finn gazed at Lilly, at the way sun filtered through the café's tinted front windows, bathing her in lavender. Lord, she was beautiful. Lord, he wanted to fulfill his husbandly duty. But no matter how much he wanted to take Lilly into his arms, there was that matter of her having been hired by Mitch to consider. Not to mention his vow to never, *ever,* get mixed up with another conniving woman.

"Finn? You there? Talk to me, man."

"I'm here. I...oh hell, bottom line, something's happening to me, Matt. I thought this was a joke. You know, to get back at Mitch, but I don't know. Once I won the bet, I figured she'd fess up that Mitch hired her, but she hasn't. And I feel kinda funny when I look at her. And when she talks, I sometimes have a hard time breathing."

"Okay, first off, I'm sure if you're in Vegas, it's the dry air making you breathe funny. And second, if Mitch hired this woman, you can't be *that* attracted to her. Either she's got you under a spell, or this is merely a rebound thing from the wedding. For the sake of this discussion, we'll call it 'the Vivian Effect.'"

"Great. We have a name, but what's the solution?"

"Simple. Go with it. She likes you. You like her. I'm failing to see the problem—unless she interferes with Friday night poker."

Swell.

Finn said a quick *catch ya later* to his friend, then hung up, grumbling, "Fat lot of help you were," as he thumped his forehead against the cool chrome front of the phone.

What was he going to do?

On the one hand, Lilly was not only a hottie, but sweeter than cotton candy. She was exactly the kind of woman he'd always pictured his kids coming home to after school.

Then, as the sun was setting, he'd park his truck in the driveway and his family would all come running out the front door to greet him—a big golden lab named Rover leading the pack—followed, of course, by the three mutts he already had. His four boys would be next to tromp down the front porch stairs. And Lilly would bring up the rear, pausing at the rail, backlit by golden afternoon sun, hugging his infant daughter to her hip.

He'd always planned on having his boys first. That way they could help him keep Charlotte's boyfriends in line—oh, and Charlotte was going to be his first daughter's name. In memory of his mom. His first son would be named Edward in honor of his dad. He'd name his second daughter, Katherine—Katie for short—for his sister.

Okay, so that was the one hand. On the other, he was a fool to think, even for a second, his dreams were about to come true.

For the last time, man, Lilly was hired by your worst enemy to mess with your head. Lilly probably isn't even her real name!

"Dallas?"

Finn looked up to see *her.*

"I don't mean to invade your privacy," she said,

"but our brunch is almost ready." She capped her words with a shy, intoxicatingly pretty grin. "After being up all night, you must be starving, and well—" she ducked her gaze "—you know it's not healthy to wait too long between meals."

As if watching himself in a movie, Finn heard the low din of conversation, the chink of silverware against china, the sad strains of a country song playing over hidden speakers. He smelled cigarette smoke and bacon and the sticky sweet scent of maple syrup. And while he was acutely aware of all that, he tried not to be aware of his ridiculous curiosity as to what it might be like to start a family with this woman who *might* be named Lilly.

Cautiously he slipped his arm about her wisp of a waist, gazing deep into her baby blues. Matt's words skipped through his brain. *She likes you. You like her. What's the problem?*

"Dallas? Are you already feeling weak?" She stood on her tiptoes, skimming cool fingers across Finn's fevered forehead. "You're hot."

For you.

"Maybe we should get you to the motel so you can lie down?"

"You want me to *lie* down, huh?" Steering her toward their table, he held her deliciously tightly.

"Watch it, mister. You know what I mean. You look sick."

"Gee, thanks."

They'd left the dark hall to enter the maze of tables and he took her by the hand to lead her through.

"Congratulations," called out a portly man seated

at the counter as they passed. "Have y'all been married long?"

Lilly beamed. "Almost an hour."

"Well, that's just great. Good luck to you both." To Finn he said, "Take care of this little missy. I can tell just by lookin' at her she's a special gal."

"Um, thanks." Finn hardly even slowed on his way to their table.

"Dallas?" she complained once they slid into their booth. "Why didn't you stop and say something to that man? He was being nice."

He sighed. "Sorry. I guess after our long night I didn't feel up to small talk."

"You *are* sick, aren't you?"

"No. Really, I feel fine."

"Then why do you seem different?"

"You're overreacting, *Mrs. Lebeaux.* I'm just tired."

Her eyes narrowed. "Okay, then tell me who you called and what they said that's made you so glum."

Finn took a deep breath. *There you go, man. You'll never get a better chance to bring up the bet. Ask her what she's doing hooked up with a slimeball like Mitch—not to mention what it'd take to buy out her contract.*

Unfortunately, just as Finn was about to pose his question, a waitress wearing a wig that looked more like tinsel than hair stopped in front of their table. "Who ordered the Graceland Special?"

"Me," Finn said.

"Okeydoke." She slid a double cheeseburger and crinkle fries in front of him. "This must be yours," she said, setting another burger and fries in front of Lilly before stepping back and putting her hands on her hips. "Strange but true observation—the only other couple I know who order burgers for breakfast has been married over sixty years. You two have that same look about you—the one that says you just might go the distance."

"Thank you," Finn's bride gushed, pressing her hands to glowing cheeks. "Including the minister who married us, you're the third person this morning to wish us luck, and you know what they say about the third time being a charm."

"Oh, so then this is your third marriage?" There was barely a rise in the waitress's purple eyebrows.

"Um, no," Lilly said with a cute frown.

Finn hid his grin behind his burger.

"I, um, meant you were the third person to wish us luck on *this* marriage."

"Oh, sure." The waitress sagely nodded. "That's great. Oh—and hey," She reached into the pocket of her short black skirt to draw out two slips of red paper. "Before I forget—The King, also known as my boss, Kenny, gives these to all our newlyweds."

"What are they?" Lilly asked, accepting their gift.

"Complimentary tickets to the matinee performance of Elvis's Bird and Dog Show. You'll love it."

"Yo, Moonbeam!" a burly bald man called from across the room. "My hair's not grownin' any thicker waitin' on you!"

"Keep your pants on, Burt. I'm comin'." To Lilly and Finn, *Moonbeam* said, "Enjoy the show," before heading Burt's way.

"Wasn't she sweet?" Lilly said. "And what fun we'll have with these tickets. A bird and dog show. How exciting. I wonder if the animals perform together?"

Finn suppressed what had to be his hundredth groan of the morning. "As newlyweds, don't we have something else we're supposed to be doing?"

"Don't tell me you mean…you know…" Her cheeks turned a dozen shades of pink.

"Yeah, that's what I mean. So? Doesn't that sound like more fun?"

"Dallas," she scolded. Lowering her voice, she said, "You know my feelings on that subject. I think it'd be best if we got to know each other first." She looked at the tickets, then her watch. "The show starts at noon. It's ten past eleven, which means if we're going to check into the motel first—*just* to guarantee our room and change our clothes—then we'd better hurry up and eat."

Ooh, you're smooth. What an amazing stroke of luck the way Lilly had managed to wriggle her ripe little tush out of sealing their vows just yet.

"This tastes delicious," she said, swallowing a bite of her burger. "I can't stand eggs, so when I was a kid, I told Mom that as soon as I grew up, I was only eating hamburgers for breakfast."

"Are you kidding?"

"No. Why would I make something like that up?"

"I wasn't implying you would, it's just that I feel the same way about eggs—or any breakfast food for that matter. I always figured why not skip breakfast and go straight to lunch." What Finn didn't reveal was that the reason he'd adopted the habit of skipping breakfast was to make the days after losing his parents and sister pass faster. If he jumped right out of bed and went straight to lunch, in a kid's mind, that translated to a lot fewer hours in the day.

His wife sat her *Love Me Tender* special down and flashed him one of her wavering grins that typically preceded tears. "Do you know what our both liking burgers for breakfast means?" Her big blue eyes turned shimmery.

I know what it usually means when you start up your sprinklers. You get whatever you want. But not this time. I'm onto you. I'm—

"It means that we really *do* have a shot at our marriage lasting forever. Everyone knows the more things a couple has in common, the more likely they are to stay together. My oldest brother, David, is a marriage counselor, so believe me, I've heard this from a reliable source. Uh…" She wiped tears from the corners of her eyes. "I'm sorry. I've been so hormonal since—well, you know. Anyway—" she reached across the table for his hands "—all I wanted to say is that Dallas Lebeaux, you are my knight in shining armor for rescuing me not only from the Wayne Newton Chapel, but—no, I'm not going to get emotional again. I just want you to know that if it's the last thing I do, I'll never make you sorry for marrying me."

"AND NOW, ladies and gentle*man*…"

Lilly grinned to see Dallas squirm at Elvis's mention of him being the only other man in the room. And what a room it was. The so-called theater had been set

up in an old grocery store. The checkouts were piled
high with souvenir T-shirts, mugs and key chains and
the raised center deli section was now a stage. The
overhead lights had been turned out and the entire pe-
rimeter of the massive space glowed with neon out-
lines of dancing pork chops and milk jugs. The place
smelled like a cross between salami and glazed donuts,
both of which made Lilly's stomach growl.

"For my next amazing feat," Elvis said, "I'll need
a lovely assistant. Do I have anyone out there who'd
like to help Sparky the Wonder Dog?"

"Me! Me!" A half dozen pint-size girls squirmed
in their seats, itching for the chance to clamber up on
stage.

"Hmm, such a tough choice," Elvis said, "You're
all so lovely, but I pick…you." He pointed to the only
one of the girls not squirming, a pigtailed angel seated
in a wheelchair. "Sir," Elvis said, pointing to Dallas.
"Could you please help the little lady onto the stage?
Her mama looks like she's got her hands full."

Lilly followed the magician's gaze to where the
girl's mother cradled a tiny bundle of blue. What a
cute baby! But then Lilly caught sight of her groom
staring at the infant and found a whole new meaning
for cute. Beaming at the tiny face, Dallas's expression
had turned to pure mush.

Wow…her heart felt ready to burst.

She'd been terrified that, because he hadn't asked
the smallest question about her baby, Dallas had
changed his mind about wanting to become a father,
but seeing him now, gazing upon a stranger's infant,
then taking extraordinary care wheeling the girl toward

the stage, Lilly again had her decision to marry him confirmed.

"There you go, sir," Elvis said. "Wheel that darling right on up the ramp, then you can take your seat."

For Lilly, with Dallas back beside her, the rest of the show passed in a blur of jumping toy poodles, squawking parrots and barely contained tears. Never could she remember having been so happy. With the help of the Internet, she'd found a wonderful father for her child.

Yes, but what about a wonderful husband for you?

She swallowed hard and cast a glance Dallas's way.

No. No matter how many times as a young woman she'd dreamed of Prince Charming sweeping her off her feet, she had to keep in mind that, now, it would simply never happen. The current platonic arrangement she shared with Dallas was beneficial for them both. If she were to open herself up to the kind of pipe dreams that had led to her involvement with Elliot, she'd only be inviting more trouble into her life.

All that said, Dallas seemed to be getting a genuine kick out of not so much watching the show, but watching how much the children around him enjoyed the show. Meeting this one-in-a-million man had been a miracle, and while she knew their feelings would never move beyond friendship, at the moment she very much felt that she had already made a lifelong friend. And somehow, she thought, swallowing past the lump in her throat, that would be enough.

She and Dallas laughed at the same corny jokes, she adored his taste in flowers and rings, they'd even eaten the same unconventional breakfast. By the time Sparky the Wonder Dog was readying for his brave fire leap and her husband had taken her hand in his, Lilly no longer felt sorry for herself, but more like the luckiest woman alive.

All too soon the show was over and they were the last to leave the small theater. While Dallas made a quick run to the rest room, she waited for him in the foyer, counting the seconds to his return.

When he strolled out of the makeshift lobby wearing a cheesy grin, she said, "What are you up to? You look like you've been doing a lot more than going to the bathroom."

He shrugged and slipped his hands into his pockets, where she could have sworn she detected the sound of crinkling plastic.

"Dallas Lebeaux, what are you hiding?"

He kissed the tip of her nose. "Can't a guy keep a secret from his wife?"

"Did you buy me a present?"

Again, all she got from him was a maddening shrug, then, "Guess you'll have to wait and see."

"Hmm, sounds intriguing." She didn't press him further, for if there was anything she liked more than her new husband, it was surprises!

"Whoa, it's bright out here," Finn said, holding the door open for his adorable wife as they moved from the dark ex-grocery store to blinding midday sun.

"It sure is." On the way to the car, she brought her hand to her forehead to shade her eyes. Sunbeams shot through the paste diamond in her gumball-machine ring, reminding him for a second of the antique ruby and diamond he'd almost slipped on Vivian's hand. The ring had been his grandmother's, then his mother's. Giving that ring to Vivian would have been the worst mistake of his life.

But then if marrying his real fiancée would have been *just* a mistake, what did marrying a hired fiancée amount to? Full-out catastrophe?

He eyed the scooped neck of the pink T-shirt Lilly had changed into. No catastrophe there. The full upper curve of her breasts peeked at him, practically sending him an engraved invitation to feel how soft they were and pliable and—

"Wasn't that girl you helped onstage adorable?"

"What? Huh?" Finn, reaching to unlock, then open Lilly's car door, was still focused on the adult entertainment.

"Don't tell me you already forgot her corkscrew pigtails?" she said, climbing inside the car.

Hell no, he hadn't forgotten the girl or her baby brother. It was just that the topic of kids was too painful to bring into this lark he and Lilly called a marriage.

"You're going to make a great father," she said after he slid behind the wheel. "My brother says you can tell a good parent by their patience, and what with all my blubbering last night and the church thing this morning—" she transfixed him with her near-flood-stage baby blues "—what can I say? You're a patient guy. A guy I know is going to make a great dad."

Talk about hitting below the belt. How had Mitch known Finn yearned to be a father? The power Lilly wielded with her body already had Finn losing control. If she started talking babies, too, he'd be a goner.

Figuring the best way to avoid the issue was to ignore it, he started the car.

"Where to?" he said.

"Want to go back to the motel and talk?"

"Nah," he said, backing out of their parking space. "It's too early for *talking*. How about playing a few slots?"

Chapter Four

"Come on, baby... Mommy needs a new pair of shoes." Lilly pulled the one-armed bandit's lever, then watched in disgust as once again, her nickel investment paid a dividend of exactly squat.

"You're not doing so hot," Mr. I-Can't-Lose said smugly from his stool beside her. His coin tray was heaped with nickels to the point that he'd had to get one of the jumbo-sized SlotWorld coin cups to hold his overflow. And wouldn't you know it? Just as she looked his way, his machine hit triple blue sevens *again.*

"Awesome!" he shouted. "That's twenty more bucks! I'm rich!"

Great. You're rich and the chink, chink, chink of nickels spewing out of your machine is giving me a headache. As were the dinging bells of other winning machines—not to mention the cigar cloud haze from the old guy on the next row.

Sighing, Lilly reached into her wallet for another five-dollar bill to slip into the change portion of the machine.

"You know, beautiful," Dallas said with an annoyingly warm smile, "you're welcome to grab a handful of my nickels."

"Thanks, but I've never been too keen on accepting charity."

"We're married. What's mine is yours." Before she could stop him, he dumped his coin cup into the base of her machine.

"Hey, what'd you do that for?" He was still leaning into her personal space and suddenly she was far more disturbed by his oh-so-male scent than his nickels.

"I did that," he said, leaving his stool to straddle her knees, "because you need to loosen up. This is our honeymoon for heaven's sake and here you are worrying more about beating a stupid slot machine than getting to know your husband."

Lilly gulped. She'd only imagined the heat of his breath on her chest, right? "Um, Dallas…" she managed to say though her lungs felt strangely weak. "I, ah, think you should get back to your own stool. Someone might take your machine."

He flashed her a wicked grin before glancing down one way, then the other of their dead-end aisle. "Looks to me like we've got the whole place to ourselves. Hmm, whatever shall we do with all this privacy?" He slipped his hands to her waist, shocking her with a sudden turn of the tables that put him back on his own stool, landing with her on his lap.

She took a long time drawing her next breath, praying the additional air might still her frenzied pulse. Rats. No such luck. "Dallas, please…"

"Please what?" he said, his breath hot against her neck, her right ear. "Please, kiss you? Please slide my hands up your shirt? Please take you back to our poor, lonely suite?"

Without waiting for her reply, he did slip his hands under her shirt, and such was her shock—not to mention secret, aching delight—she froze, allowing him to skim his open palms up her torso until finally reaching her silk-covered breasts. The heat of his palms caused her nipples to traitorously swell, and she deeply, honestly searched for a reason to push him away. But in the end, the only dizzying thought that sprang to mind was that Dallas was now her husband. She was his wife. And if they stayed their current course, no matter how impossible it seemed, every dream she'd ever had would be well on its way to coming true.

Skimming her hands to his back, she arched into him, licking her lips before darting her gaze to make one last check they were alone. However wary she might have been about ever again opening her heart, the attraction drawing her ever-closer to her husband was a powerful thing. Two seconds later, when Dallas still hadn't crushed his lips to hers, she decided to live life on the edge by cupping the back of his head and drawing him to her, finishing the job herself.

Dear Lord, Finn thought on the heels of a groan. Had he ever partaken of a woman so sweet? Lilly's kisses tasted like ice cream and cotton candy. Bubble gum and red hots. She was the most honeyed, most indescribably delicious thing he'd ever tasted and he couldn't wait for more. Damn Mitch. Finn had won his part of the bet fair and square. Whatever happened between Lilly and him from this point on was gravy— or maybe that should have been chocolate sauce!

"Oh, Dallas," she softly crooned. "You have such a way with kisses."

Screech. There went those damned mental brakes.

Like fingernails on a chalkboard, Lilly's calling him Dallas grated his nerves. That's it. Once and for all, they had to establish the perimeters of their relationship—not that they even had a relationship—but before he made love to her, which he fully planned to do by the end of the day, Finn wanted to hear *his* name spilled from those full, pouty lips.

"Um, Lilly," he said, summoning superhero strength to push her even slightly away. "We need to talk."

"We will," she said, marching a parade of kisses down his neck. "Later."

"I know, but don't you think we should talk now?"

Kiss, kiss. "Now that you taught me how much fun kissing can be, I'd much rather kiss now, and talk later."

Dear Lord. She ducked to kiss his collarbone and the indentation at the base of his throat. She was absolutely right. Now was not the time to talk. Now was the time to stand up, tuck Lilly's legs around his waist and march to the nearest utility closet to finish what this minx had started. Well, technically he'd started this particular escapade, but then at this point, who was going to call him on a technicality? Yep, without a doubt, now was the time to—

"Excuse me," said a graveled voice from behind him. "Are these machines taken?"

Finn looked up.

An elderly couple walked in their direction. They

each had spiky gray hair and matching T-shirts that read Alta Vista Seniors Rock!

He groaned.

Lilly giggled. "Nope," she said to the man. "Use any of them you want."

"Way to go," Finn muttered in his bride's ear. "And this was just getting good."

"Shame on you," she said, eyes sparkling. "After our agreeing to take things slow, you did realize my kisses weren't going any further, didn't you? I'm a good girl. I would never even consider indulging in a serious public display of affection."

"Right. After what we just shared, you're a good girl my—"

"Oops…better watch that language." She pressed her fingers to his lips.

"Woman." He gave her saucy behind a light smack before hefting her back to her own stool. "Either sit there and play nice, or I'm going to take you back to our suite and ravage you senseless. What's it going to be?"

Already knowing her answer, Finn scooped the nickels in his machine into a plastic coin bucket.

"What are you doing?" she asked.

He froze. "What's it look like I'm doing? We're going back to our suite ASAP, right?"

"Wrong. You gave me two choices, remember? And I choose to stay here and play. After all," she said, glancing toward her meager pile of coins. "I have a lot of catching up to do, don't you think?"

"No. What I think is that—"

"Oh look, there's a waitress and I am kind of hungry. Ma'am?" she called out with a friendly wave.

"Could you please bring me some popcorn and a Shirley Temple?"

THREE HOURS' WORTH of slot-playing later, in a mall attached to the casino, Lilly asked Dallas, "Tell me again why you didn't think to pack a suitcase for our honeymoon?" Her words barely rose above the sound of a barbershop quartet competing with the food court's waterfall.

"I did pack," he said, "but I didn't think to bring my bag to Lu's."

"Lu's? Is that what you locals call Luigi's?"

"Yep."

A trio of belly-ring-baring teens passed by, nearly running Lilly into an ivy-filled planter in their blatant ogling of her husband.

"That was rude," she said after they passed.

"What?" Dallas glanced over his shoulder. "I didn't see them do anything."

"You wouldn't."

"Great. A department store," he said, veering to the right. "I'm a one-stop-shopping kind of guy."

Grasping her hand, he towed her through the mirror-and-glass cosmetic section with all its exotic scents and women, and again Lilly noticed how much attention *her* husband was receiving.

"Evenin', ladies," he said to a pair of sleek brunettes standing behind the Chanel counter. "Nice place you have here."

"Thanks," the taller one said. "Come back and see us when you can stay a while." The woman then had the nerve to pucker up her big, harlot-red lips and blow Dallas a kiss.

A kiss!

"Did you see that?" Lilly complained under her breath.

"No, what'd I miss this time?"

While the two thoroughbreds ducked their heads together and snickered, Lilly slipped her arm around Dallas's waist, making sure her left-hand ring finger—along with its ring—was visible. Honestly, what was this world coming to? Couldn't those two find their own men?

"Did you have to be so polite?" she said, hoping it was overwrought pregnancy hormones and not too many kisses that had brought out this sudden possessive streak.

"Sure, I did. Mama taught me to be polite to all the ladies—" he leaned close enough to finish his sentence in Lilly's ear "—especially the pretty ones. Like you." Before stepping onto the down escalator, he finished his flattery with an enchanting kiss to her cheek.

Wow. Wow. Wow. With a hundred years of composition time, Dallas couldn't have thought of a more perfect comeback. Oh, she knew her breakup with Elliot was far too fresh for her to even think about falling for another man, but honestly, how was she supposed to resist Dallas? He was charming and kind and honest and dependable. No wonder so many women found him tempting.

"What do you think of these?" Finn asked a few minutes later, in front of a rack of khakis, cursing Vivian for locking his suitcase in her car. Probably by the time he got back, her folks would have retrieved her yellow Mustang from the church parking lot and dumped his suitcase in the Lost River. After she'd taken off with Mr. Motorcycle, they'd actually scolded Finn for not chasing after her and bringing her back!

"Khakis are nice. I imagine you get tired of wearing a suit to work every day, huh?"

He frowned. "A suit?" Boy, Mitch had done a lousy job on the dossier he'd given Lilly, but that was all right.

Tonight Finn had big plans, starting with buying a new set of duds, then taking his bride out for a nice dinner, at the end of which he'd force her to come clean or stick her with the bill. Okay, so he probably wouldn't stick her with the bill, but for the hell she'd put his swollen nether regions through that afternoon, the least she could do was pay for his meal.

"Yeah, you know, a suit. As in three-piece or monkey?"

He grinned. "Let's just say Monsieur Levi is my favorite tailor."

She flashed him a funny look before moving on to the next rack. "This is nice," she said, showing him an emerald-green Polo pullover. Holding it to his chest, she added, "Perfect. This color looks great with your eyes."

"You like it, huh?"

She nodded.

"Great. Put it in the cart."

"We don't have a cart, remember? They're all back at the Elvis show holding Sparky the Wonder Dog T-shirts."

"Right," he said with a laughing groan. "How could I forget?"

She wrapped her arms around him in a spontaneous hug, and for an instant, holding her with the shirt she'd selected caught between them, everything in the world felt right. Time stood still and all that mattered was Lilly. Lilly sharing his love of hamburgers for breakfast. Lilly laughing beside him while Elvis coaxed a bunch of poodles and parrots into barking and squawking "Don't Be Cruel." Lilly, kissing him on a slot-machine stool, making him feel like the luckiest—not to mention randiest—man alive.

"We're starting to have quite a shared history," she said shyly, pulling away to move on to the next rack of shirts.

"Oh yeah?"

"Just think of all we've managed to squeeze into one day. Sheesh, the last guy I dated barely even took me out for dinner before he was expecting me to fall into his bed."

Finn narrowed his eyes. "How did that make you feel?"

"How do you think? Awful. All I wanted was a piece of Elliot's time, but in the end, all I got was a piece of him."

"What do you mean?"

She ducked her gaze. "You know."

No, I don't, and he was itching like hell to ask, but couldn't—or maybe *wouldn't*—would be the more correct term. A second ago, when she'd held up that shirt to his chest, they'd felt cozy again, like a couple, just like when she tied his bow tie at their first attempt at a wedding. But knowing her capacity for deceit, he knew better than to step any further into her spell.

She was an enchantress, weaving a powerful potion about his senses. He knew better than to fall for her, yet every time he smelled her floral perfume, he felt a little more lost. If she had been any other woman, that fact would have thrilled him. But she was hooked up with Mitch, and the day Vivian left him, Finn had promised himself to never, ever get mixed up with another conniving woman.

"What size do you wear in jeans and I'll grab you a pair of 501s," she said, evidently as happy to change the subject as he was.

"Thirty-four thirty-six. Thanks." Finn felt like a dope for not asking her more about this Elliot character. Even though Lilly was hooked up with Mitch, she deserved better than the kind of second-rate treatment her last guy had given.

Trailing after her, he wondered how she knew he wore 501s. He wished she'd known by some kind of powerful ESP thing they had going between them, but alas, the fact that she knew what kind of jeans he wore could only mean one thing—Mitch had finally gotten one of his facts right.

Once they selected and purchased slacks, jeans, a couple T-shirts and boxers—even a new belt and shoes—Finn changed from his tux to Lilly's green shirt and the khakis, then guided his bride back out into the mall.

In front of the waterfall, the barbershop quartet had been replaced by a group of elementary kids singing "How Much Is That Doggy in the Window?" The sight of them, not to mention their boisterous sound, caused his heart to ache. He wanted to start a family so much, which just made Lilly's deception harder to bear.

If only she were the ultralovable kissing angel she portrayed. Unfortunately, it was anyone's guess who she really was. For all he knew, she could be a professional con artist—available for hire on the Web at Scams-R-Us.com.

"Aren't they cute?" she said, holding her tummy with a misty look in her eyes. "And they're doing such a great job. Their parents must be so proud."

"Yep." If he talked about kids any more his heart would bust in two. Time to get back to business. "How about me taking you out to a swanky Italian place for dinner?"

Her eyes lit up. "Sounds great, but…" Her grin fell.

"But what?"

"All I brought is shorts and jeans. Remember how you said we wouldn't be doing anything fancy?"

"Right, because I wanted to *buy* you something fancy. Come on," he said, patting himself on the back for quick thinking. "Let's go find the dress of your dreams."

That brought back her smile. "You, sir, certainly know how to charm a girl."

"Hey, they don't—" It'd been on the tip of his tongue to brag that people didn't call him "Lucky" Finn Reilly for nothing when it occurred to him that they were still playing the Dallas charade. Damn, damn and double damn. Well, because he was having such a great time, he'd let this farce continue until dinner, but over a nice bottle of Chardonnay, whether Lilly liked it or not, she was going to confess to the part she'd played in the bet.

"Don't what?" Lilly asked, pausing in front of a store window loaded with dresses.

"Nothing. I forgot what I was going to say."

Oblivious to the battle raging in his head, she

flashed him her prettiest grin. "Don't you hate it when that happens?" Her attention back to the dresses, she said, "Which one do you think would look best?"

Why did women do this? Vivian had asked this sort of question with her shoes and, invariably, when he chose the pair he honestly thought looked best, she called him hopeless. Told him he wouldn't recognize a good-looking shoe if it jumped up and kicked him on his—well, anyway, she hadn't valued his fashion opinion.

"Dallas? I'm waiting."

"Um, I like..." He dropped his voice to a mumble.

"Which one?" The children's choir launched into a number about Martians and car horns beep-beeping. "I couldn't hear you over the kids."

Oh hell, he might as well tell her the truth and get his scolding over with. "I like the simple black one. It looks like that silky fabric would feel good against your skin...and mine." He flashed her his most devilish grin.

"Oh, Dallas!" Flinging her arms around his neck, she gushed, "What are the odds that out of all those dresses, you'd choose the exact same one as me?"

"I did?" He gulped. "Yeah, well, I suppose that's easy for you to say now."

Stepping away from him, she placed her hands on her hips. "Dallas Lebeaux, have you no faith in your fashion sense? That dress is amazing. Any woman would be thrilled to wear it." Grabbing him by the hand, she towed him into the store. "Come on, I want to see if it fits."

FROM INSIDE a fuchsia dressing room that had black feathers lining the ceiling, Lilly peeked between the door slats to see Dallas seated on a hot-pink velvet love seat. Ricky Martin crooned a love song over hidden speakers and the air was thick with rose-scented potpourri. Never had a man looked more out of place or ill at ease, yet there her husband sat, patiently waiting for his personal fashion show.

After slipping off her shorts and T-shirt, Lilly drew the cool black silk over her head, shoulders, breasts and hips, then surveyed her image in the mirror. Wow. The garment clung in all the right places and none of the wrong. It did show far more cleavage than she'd thought she had, but seeing as she was now a married woman, she figured it wouldn't hurt to give her husband a thrill.

After fluffing her hair and applying fresh lipstick, Lilly was ready for her one-woman show.

"Taa-daa," she finally said, throwing open the dressing-room door.

Bull's-eye.

Dallas's slightly dazed expression was exactly what she'd been aiming for. "What do you think?" she asked, knowing full well she looked better than she ever had.

"What I think," he said, clutching his chest, "is that you're trying to do your old man in for the life insurance. Seriously, woman. You look hot."

Chapter Five

"So there we were," Lilly said later that evening over fettuccine Alfredo at Vicienti's Ristorante. "My best friend, Gail, and I were tossing this diving brick around in the locker room. Swim practice was over, but Gail's dad had called our coach to tell him he'd be late. So anyway, we knew we had plenty of time to head out to the parking lot, so we figured why not start a game of locker-room catch? All was going great until I slipped on a wet spot on the tile and the brick went flying straight into one of the sinks. Crash. The porcelain shattered in at least a hundred pieces."

"Oh, man, what'd you do?" Finn asked, entranced not only by Lilly's latest story of her childhood mis-adventures, but her captivating features. Candlelight made her skin glow honey-gold and her natural-blond curls kissed blushing cheeks. Her eyes had become inviting seas of blue and no matter how hard Finn tried convincing himself she was the enemy, he feared he was falling for her.

Though the restaurant was crowded, their corner table might as well have been their own private paradise. Roaming violinists played Italian love songs and the air smelled ripe with tomatoes, fresh baked bread, and an aromatic bouquet of herbs.

"What'd we do?" Lilly repeated, filling his soul with her silvery laugh. "What we did was run like the devil. That night, I stayed over at Gail's and we thought we were home free—at least until, unbeknownst to us, our coach called her father. What we hadn't realized—duh—was that since we were the only two left in the locker room, we were the only kids who could have been to blame for the broken sink. Thank goodness, my folks were out of town that weekend and my brother, Mark, on vacation from law school, pretended to be Dad so I wouldn't get in trouble."

Finn frowned. "So if Mark covered for you, what kind of lesson did you learn?"

"Well..." Clouds passed over her sky-blue eyes and she nibbled on her full, lower lip. "I guess at that time I didn't learn much of anything, other than to be grateful for my quick-thinking brother. But now... since meeting you, I feel reformed."

"How's that?"

"I've finally learned to handle my own damage control. And now that I'm Mrs. Dallas Lebeaux, that whole mess with Mr. Elliot Dinsmoore has gone from being a problem to a blessing."

Reaching for a bread stick, Finn felt as if Lilly were speaking in code. Who was this Elliot Dinsmoore guy she kept bringing up? And since she was no longer with him, what kind of problem did she have? Because from where Finn was sitting, he saw that her biggest problem was being associated with Mitch.

Thoughtfully chewing, Finn figured that maybe she'd been doing so much acting that she'd somehow mixed up her roles.

"Mmm, the music is beautiful isn't it?"

"Not half as beautiful as you." Despite her being a soulless conniver, Finn couldn't take his eyes off his bride. Her eyes, her lips, her golden curls. Why did everything he thought he knew about her have to be a mirage? "Want to dance?" he asked, yet again putting off the inevitable confrontation of calling her bluff.

"I'd love to."

He stood, offered her his hand, and then they swayed as one to Italian love songs as old as time. Her so-called simple black dress dipped dramatically in the back and he couldn't resist skimming the tips of his fingers down her spine. Lilly's skin was magnolia-smooth and she smelled fresh and pure—like soap and a light shampoo that could have been sunshine in a bottle.

With a mewing sigh, she rested her cheek against his chest. Her soft curls tickled his chin. "This is nice," she said. "Makes me think we just might be one of those couples who really do live happily ever after."

He winced. Why did she keep doing this? Acting as if everything between them was as it should be?

Mitch wasn't a wealthy man. How much did she stand to gain by stringing Finn along? Shoot, for all he knew, she could be trading her services in exchange for Mitch's carpentry talents—shabby as they were.

"Dallas?"

"Yep. Our marriage is a fairy tale all right." Only he wasn't talking the typical *Cinderella* or *Beauty and the Beast,* but more of a *Draculette* with him cast as the vamp's victim!

"Ready to go back to our suite?"

"Are you?"

He felt her nod.

"Okay…" Taking her by the hand, he led her through a garden of well-dressed diners. "But do you mind if, before we go, we talk?"

The little minx answered by shyly averting her gaze. "I-if you don't mind, I'd rather go back to the motel. I never thought I'd be saying this, but after that buffet of sweet kisses you gave me this afternoon, I'm kind of hungry for dessert."

BY THE TIME they reached their suite, Lilly wondered if people died from longing?

Her one night with Elliot hadn't been any big deal. At the time, she had thought she loved him, but now she knew better. She had never loved Elliot. She'd only been lured to him by the notion of love that she'd waited her whole life to find. Now, what she felt for Dallas, while it couldn't possibly be love, was at once wild yet safe. Unnerving yet comfortable. How it was possible that, after only one day of marriage, she felt irrevocably drawn to him, she didn't know. Tonight the only thing she truly did know was that her whole life up to this point had been based upon crazy, in-calculable risks. But here, in Dallas's arms, she felt grounded and finally, wonderfully mature.

While he struggled to get the card key to work, she giggled.

He turned to her and growled.

"You'd better watch it," he said, after finally opening the door. "I've had about all of your teasing I care to take."

"Ooh, big threats. Bet you can't back 'em up with action." Inside the room, the door closed and locked behind them, she pinned him to the wall for a surprisingly hungry kiss.

"For you being a bettin' woman," he said on a groan, "you sure don't know much about knowing when to fold."

He skimmed his big hands down her bare back and when he reached her bottom, he gripped it hard, lifting her off her feet and against his arousal. Knowing he was as hot for her as she was for him only made him that much more attractive and she deepened their kiss, doing things with her tongue that she'd only read about in books.

"I've got to have you," he said. "Right here. Right now. No more games, Lilly. This is for real."

"Oh…yes…" What games he was speaking of she didn't have a clue. She'd just add his cryptic statement to the ever-growing pile of things they'd talk about in the morning. Right now, though, nothing mattered but that he'd set her on her feet.

Fingers splayed on her hips, he knelt before her, shoving up her dress, revealing her black lace panties.

"Wow," he said on a groan before kissing the barely there, center vee panel. Her blood turned to shimmering honey. Need pulsed between her legs.

He pushed her dress higher, kissed the crown of her belly and ran his tongue in agonizingly slow circles around her navel. She sliced her fingers through his hair, urging him which way she didn't know.

Higher went her dress, and then he was standing, tugging it all the way over her head. The silky garment caught on her left earring. Keeping his touch tender, he separated the fabric from the gold stem, swearing softly under his breath when the task took longer than expected.

Exposed to the room's nighttime chill, her braless nipples puckered and hardened. From somewhere in the depths of the mighty Mount Vesuvius, red light glowed, reminding her, when her husband took her hardened bud into his mouth, of how close she was to the first of her own personal eruptions.

He moved his kisses to her throat and she arched her head, granting him access to all he desired. "Please…" she said, not sure what she was begging for but knowing, whatever it was, she wanted it to come soon.

Her fingers at the button to his slacks, she nimbly undid it, then slid down his fly. "Come on. Just like you said. Right here. Right now."

He stopped, curved his fingers around her throat, planting his thumb beneath her chin. Searching her eyes, he said, "You're sure?"

"Yes. I need you inside me." *To prove what I'm feeling isn't a dream.*

It took only seconds for him to tear his shirt over his head and toss it to the floor beside her dress. Another second for him to rip the side strings of her fragile panties. "Oops," he said, holding up the wisp of fabric as if it were a prize. "Guess I didn't realize my own strength."

"I did," she said with a knowing smile, skimming her hands up his sculpted chest.

He tossed what was left of her panties to the growing pile of clothes, then once again was lifting her, only this time, he urged her knees around his waist.

"What about your pants?" she asked, entwining her arms about his neck.

"What pants?" With a wink and simple shifting of his boxers, he released himself. One swift, sure thrust later, she sighed when her body swallowed him whole.

Sweating, panting, she clung to him while over and over he thrust and pressure built. She kissed his ear and neck and when the spellbinding torture became too great, she bit his shoulder, frenzied from need.

Higher and higher her spirit soared, and always, just when she felt near the top of a towering peak, there was another mountain to climb, another icy, hot cliff to scale.

She pressed her fingertips into his back, bracing for the elemental rush awaiting her at the top. "Yes," she cried. "Oh, yes, yes, yes…" And then she was there, at the summit, and all around her, sun exploded and angels sang and if only for that instant, her life reached the pinnacle of perfection.

FINN AND HIS BRIDE were lounging in the eerie red glow of the bubbling crater Jacuzzi when she asked, "When you were a kid, what was your favorite game to play?"

"That's a tough question." Especially since she was naked against him, running her short pink nails in slow circles through the hair on his chest. Feeling himself swelling all over again, he tried to stay focused. "Let's see, Monopoly was fun. And playing Matchbox cars." He took another second to think. "But I guess my favorite game would have had to be playing explorer. The area where I grew up had an old silver mine we weren't supposed to mess around in, but did anyway. About a quarter mile down into one of the tunnels, the miner's shaft opened into a cave that was a real freak of nature. There was even a small lake. A gang of us guys would go down there with lanterns and play pirate, or gold miners, or jungle explorer—didn't really matter what the theme was. We always had a good time."

"That does sound fun." She kissed an indentation in his shoulder.

"Come to think of it," he said, gazing at their surroundings, "this suite reminds me of that old cave."

The walls and ceiling had been rounded, then coated in bumpy concrete to resemble the inside of a lava tube. The bed consisted of a huge multileveled platform upon which piles of plush pillows and fake fur rugs had been artfully strewn.

On the wall across from the bed roared a gas log fire—okay, so it might not have exactly roared, but it was putting out a fair amount of light and heat.

"Did you ever take any girls down there with you?"

"One. Her name was Shannon Jowoskiwitz and she waited until after we hiked all the way down to tell me she was afraid of the dark. So, here I'd set up this big seduction scene. You know, mixed up a canteen of extrasugary cherry Kool-Aid, snitched a whole box of saltines, and the second we got to my favorite rock where I planned to wow her with a kiss, she freaked and demanded I show her the passage out.''

"I'm sorry," his bride said, and because the mood was right, Finn believed her. "Did she give you a kiss once you brought her back outside?"

"Nah, by then she said she was late for dinner and had to hurry home."

A thoughtful expression lingering on her face, Lilly said, "I've never been afraid of the dark."

"Oh?" Finn placed his hands on her hips and drew her up the length of him for a long, wet kiss. "What else aren't you afraid of?"

"Mmm, not spiders. And I've never been afraid of—" her eyes sparkled with mischief as her fingers dallied beneath the red bubbles "—big snakes."

Finn gasped when she grabbed hold of him and gave him a squeeze. "Ouch. Do you know what you're playing with, little girl?"

"Only my favorite new toy."

That was all the cue Finn needed to take this game to a naughty new level. With a swoosh, he rose from the water, scooping his bride along with him.

"What are you doing?" she protested laughingly, kicking her legs while he headed for the lowest level of the bed, which was only a few feet from the fire.

"What do you think I'm doing? I'm playing explorer and you're my captured native."

"That's not politically correct," she said with a teasing tsk-tsk.

"Okay," he said, gently setting her on the faux-fur-covered platform and placing a leopard-print pillow beneath her head. "How about if I pay you to be my captive?"

She pretended to look shocked. "That's even worse. Then I'd be like your concubine."

"Yes," he said, eyeing her before kneeling at her side to draw one hardened nipple into his mouth. "But you'd be my *favorite* concubine. And you know, along with favored status always comes special privileges."

"Like wha—" Before she could finish the question, he skimmed his fingertips along her abdomen and between her legs.

"Open sesame," he said, "And we shall see what treasures await us deep inside the sultan's secret cavern."

On a breathless giggle, she did as he asked, only to quickly realize he wasn't finding treasure but creating it. As if an invisible drum beat deep within her, with his fingers and tongue he established a rhythm old as time. Suddenly she was no longer Lilly, but the exotic chief of a long-forgotten nubile tribe.

"I—I think I like this game," she said, her breath coming in ragged spurts.

"Me, too." Like a stealthy jungle cat caught lapping forbidden cream, he looked up and shot her a lethally handsome grin. In the dancing firelight, his dark eyes shone obsidian and his skin was slick with sweat. Heat was building.

In the room.

In her body.

In her soul.

He brought her to climax again and again, and then he was again inside her, only this time, instead of him supporting her weight, she supported him, meeting him thrust for deeper thrust.

Their strange, glowing environment transported them to another time and place when there were no societal rules because there was no society.

They made up their own rules as they went along and fleeting words like *wild* and *unbridled* and *carnal* sprang to Lilly's fevered mind. They licked and nipped, and when exhaustion claimed them, their mating turned softer, sweeter, to touching and whispering and mewing indecipherable yet universally acknowledged words of affection.

Sated, they lay side by side, stroking each other's face and hair.

Right before his eyes, Finn watched as Lilly closed her eyes and drifted into a deep sleep. He instinctively thought to cover her, but the fire's warmth made the idea of using a blanket silly. Tropical heat encased them both, and Finn was in danger of drowsing off as well. The problem was, he didn't want to sleep, not when he was terrified of waking and discovering that this dream woman he knew as Lilly was gone.

In her place would be the real woman Mitch had hired.

Her name would be Sheila or Kimberly, and she wouldn't be soft, but hard as nails, capable of carrying out even this elaborate a hoax for nothing more than a little cash and the knowledge that she'd played him for a fool.

When he could no longer force himself to keep his eyes open, he let them fall closed, but even then, his last thought before losing consciousness was of her.

Of Lilly.

And of the question, how was he going to let her go?

LILLY WOKE SLOWLY, aware of every deliciously sore muscle in her body. Beside her, her husband softly snored.

To the right of the bed, sunbeams shafted through a tiny part in the red flame-patterned curtains, alerting her to the fact that morning had indeed come. What a wild and wonderful night. What a radical departure from the way she'd thought she would be spending it!

Frowning, it dawned on Lilly that no matter how incredibly attracted she was to her husband, a repeat performance of what she and Dallas shared must never happen. For if she spent too much more time in his arms, she was terrified of going that next step further, which was wanting him in her heart. And after the Elliot mess, opening herself up to another relationship simply wouldn't work.

Careful not to wake Dallas, she lifted his arm from where he'd draped it around her waist, then slid out from under him.

In the bathroom, she used the facilities, took a steamy shower, then fished through her suitcase for fresh, albeit slightly rumpled, green shorts and a white T-shirt.

She'd just brushed her teeth when it occurred to her how hungry she was. Knowing a delicious room-service breakfast was only a phone call away, she rummaged through a faux-fur-trimmed desk drawer for the menu, then ordered cheeseburgers and fries for two, along with ice water and carafes of both regular and decaf coffee.

By the time she'd finished blow-drying and curling her hair and applying light makeup, a knock sounded at the door.

On her way to answer it, she glanced at the platform they'd used as a bed, not surprised to find Dallas still fast asleep—not to mention naked as the day he was born. The sight of his sculpted body and the memory of how he'd used it to bring her a glorious amount of pleasure temporarily muddled her thoughts.

What was it she was supposed to be doing?

Another knock, this time harder, rattled the door.

Oh yeah. Breakfast.

She tossed a light blanket over Dallas's sleeping form, then, as the waiter knocked for a third time, she sang out, "Coming!"

"Hey," said a clean-shaven guy in his early twenties from behind a loaded white-clothed cart. "Did you order room service?"

"I sure did. Why don't you let me take it from here."

"No can do, I'm supposed to set up everything for you."

"Really, that's okay," she protested. "My husband's still sleeping."

"Oh. *Ooh.*"

While the kid blushed, Lilly commandeered the cart, capably steering it into the room. "If you'll wait a second, I'll get you a tip." Assuming she could find her purse.

Her gaze skittered from the floor to the bed to the desk, but it was nowhere to be found. What she did see was Dallas's wallet lying on the boulder serving as a bedside table. Figuring that since she was now his wife, he wouldn't mind if she snatched some cash, she opened it wide and drew out three ones she then handed to the waiter.

He said a quick thanks before jogging off down the hall.

Lilly had closed and locked the door and was heading back to the boulder to replace Dallas's wallet when she stumbled over her pile of luggage.

While she managed to catch herself, the wallet yawned, flying halfway across the room to land in a heap of credit cards and cash.

She had crossed over to it, stooping to gather everything into a tidy pile before sticking each card back into its respective leather slot when the name sprawled across the bottom of a credit card caught her eye. *Finnigan Reilly.*

Furrowing her eyebrows, she looked at the gas card beside the credit card. The name read *Finnigan Reilly.*

Heart pounding, hands trembling, she looked at a department store card, a library card, a blood donor card, even his tux rental ticket. All of them—every single one, read *Finnigan* or *Finn Reilly.*

Short of breath, pulse racing, she looked at her peacefully sleeping husband, then back to the wallet.

She had to find Dallas's driver's license. Surely, with all those other cards, there had to be some kind of mistake. One look at his license would clear everything up.

Wham!

As if she'd received a physical blow, her worst fear was confirmed. There, along with the official state seal of Utah, was undeniable proof. The man she had married wasn't trustworthy, mild-mannered, child-loving Dallas Lebeaux, but a total, complete—possibly even dangerous—stranger named Finn Reilly.

Lilly wanted to pull a Victorian stunt like collapsing in a fit of vapors, but she was much too strong a woman for that. Hand protectively over her womb, she marched to the stranger who had somehow become her husband and shook him as hard as she could. "Wake up!" she demanded.

"Huh? What?" He groggily came to. "What time is it?"

"It's time," she said, holding his driver's license a scant two inches from his face, "to tell me who the hell you are!"

Chapter Six

"Excuse me?" Finn said, wondering what could have turned normally mild mannered Lilly into this raving lunatic. "You know exactly who I am."

"No, I don't. I don't have a clue who you are other than a man who quite possibly kidnapped my real fiancé." After tossing his wallet in his face, she turned to the window, sobbing as if her best friend had died.

Lord Almighty, he'd had it with the acting. He'd meant to clear up this whole business about the bet long before they'd partaken of each other's many pleasures, but one thing had led to another and, well…

He'd be the first to admit that things had gotten a bit out of hand, but that was no reason for Lilly to go off on him. "Look, lady, you could win an award with all the boo-hooing you've been doing, but enough's enough. Mitch and I had a bet, fair and square, and I know you think you pulled the wool over my eyes, but you didn't. We're married, sweetheart, and I've got the license in my name to prove it."

"Stop." Lilly's head was spinning and she collapsed onto the nearest pile of faux fur. "What are you talking about? What bet? And who's Mitch?"

How could this be happening? She'd planned her marriage to Dallas so carefully, covering every possible contingency, but never the scenario where she married the wrong man!

"What do you mean, what bet?" he said, scrambling to his feet—all seventy-five gloriously naked inches of him! "You sashayed into Lu's telling me you were all ready for a wedding. You even addressed me by the wrong name to lead me off track, but I'm no fool, Lilly—if that's even your real name. I knew all along you were trying to marry me under the wrong name so Mitch could win Abigail on a technicality."

"Who's Abigail? And for the last time, who's Mitch?"

"You know damned well Abigail's my truck—the truck your boss planned to drive off in."

Now Lilly really did feel she was near fainting. The only question was whether it was a hunger faint or panic faint. Either way, she knew she didn't want to do it in front of this virtual stranger—a naked stranger! Had she really only yesterday said she liked surprises?

Reaching for a fry from the breakfast tray, she shoved it into her mouth and swallowed before ducking her head between her knees.

"What's the matter with you?" he asked.

"I'm about to pass out from the shock of all this—as if you'd even care."

"What's that supposed to mean? I'm the injured party here. All along your sole purpose in this marriage has been to scam me, and now, you've decided to play the innocent victim? I don't think so—and would you please look at me when I'm yelling at you?''

"I can't look at you. You're naked!''

"Yeah, well, that didn't seem to bother you much last night, Little Miss Game Player.''

That brought her out of her faint. "Why you...'' Storming to her feet, she pummeled her fists against his chest, but she might as well have been punching a brick wall. This Finn person was built.

As she remembered all too well in intimate detail!

Furiously blushing, she turned her back on him, but luckily she was at least facing the food tray. Reaching under the plastic lid, she snatched three more fries.

"You might save a bit of that for me,'' he said, grabbing some fries for himself. "I swear, the only other woman I've seen eat more than you was my best friend Matt's sister—and she was eight months' pregnant!''

It was on the tip of Lilly's tongue to tell this creep that she *was* pregnant, but then she decided against it. Who knew how he felt about babies, let alone the fact that she'd be having one in seven months!

"Could you *please* put some clothes on?'' she said, sharply averting her gaze. "You need to tell me who you are, but I'd appreciate you doing it fully dressed.''

"By all means, your highness. Anything else your conniving heart desires?''

"Yes.'' Her lower lip started to quiver and the back of her throat felt tight. She'd never liked fighting with her brothers and sisters and she sure wasn't enjoying this altercation with the man who claimed to be her husband. First one tear fell, rapidly followed by an-

other and another. "I—I want you to stop yelling,"
she wailed. "A-and put s-some clothes on, a-and tell
me who Mitch is…a-and—"

"Okay, okay, I get the picture." Finn put his hands
up to stop her midstream. "Just quit crying." Spying
his new jeans spilling from a nearby bag, he snatched
them out, jerked the tags off and pulled them on, all
the while feeling strangely self-conscious. Lord, he
had a tough time thinking straight when Lilly was crying, and he sure couldn't find it in his heart to stay
angry with her. What he really felt like doing was
pulling her into a hug, but that was ludicrous in light
of their current situation, which was growing stranger
by the minute.

Why did she keep asking such weird questions? If
she didn't know who Mitch was, or at the very least
who Abigail was, then what did that say about who
she was?

The question struck terror in his soul.

Sitting quietly, nibbling on a juicy-looking cheeseburger, she watched him yank the tags off a red
T-shirt and pull it over his head.

"What?" he said, his voice rougher than he'd in-
tended.

"Nothing. I'm just wondering how I could have
made such a huge mistake? I mean, I've made some
doozies over the years, but this one takes the cake.
And if you're not Dallas, then where is he?"

Finn's feeling of unease grew by a factor of ten.

"I know I would love Dallas. And he certainly
loves me."

"That's some kind of love, lady, when, if what

you're saying is true, you obviously didn't even know what the guy looks like or you wouldn't have thought I was him.''

"I've seen his fuzzy picture."

"Great. Did you ever think it might be a good idea to actually meet the man himself before you ran off to marry him?''

"We did meet. Through e-mail. And I'm not the one who did something wrong here, mister. You were the one who should have told me right from the start who you were." Flashing him a look of horror blended with disgust, she said, "At least one good thing came out of all this."

"What's that?''

"At least we're not *really* married. Because for us to be *really* married, I would have had to marry you. Which I didn't. My marriage license reads Dallas Lebeaux, and since you're obviously not him, then we're obviously not married.''

His stomach hit rock bottom. "Think again." She looked so alone and fragile, holding on to the food cart as if it were her only port in a mighty ugly storm. "Why don't you try to relax?" he said. "I'm thinking this explanation may take a while."

While he told her the details of Mitch's bet, she perched on the edge of the bed. Finished, Finn didn't know whether to be relieved or terrified that the woman he'd married was indeed named Lilly Churchill, or rather, Lilly Reilly.

"This is awful," she said with a pitiful sigh.

"Why? I know this mess would have been a whole lot easier to clean up if we hadn't..." Thoughts of exactly what they'd done caused his face to go all hot. "Well, you know what we did. Anyway, if we hadn't done that, we probably could have gotten an annulment, but now I think we'll have to go with the full-fledged divorce."

"No, no, no," she said, scrambling from the bed to furiously pace.

In the light of day, far from the pleasure den it'd been during the night, the room looked shabby—even tawdry. So, he mused, the night had been a dream after all. A dream that had turned into a genuine nightmare.

"No, we can't file for divorce this afternoon?"

"No, as in we can't file for divorce, period."

He scrunched his nose. "I'm afraid I'm not following you."

Turning her back on him, she headed for her suitcase, knelt before it and started folding like a woman possessed.

"Now isn't the time to do your laundry," Finn pointed out. "We need to be talking lawyers."

"There isn't going to be a lawyer," she said without stopping.

"I know I'm going to regret asking this, but why?"

"Because there isn't going to be a divorce. My whole life I've been either running from trouble or covering it up, but no more. Quite simply, by law—not to mention after what we did last night—we are now, for better, or in our case, worse—married. For life. *Forever.*"

"Are you nuts?" Finn asked. "We don't even know each other."

"Far from being nuts, as you so eloquently put it, I'm merely trying to make the best of a bad situation."

"So let me get this straight, you're calling being married to me a bad situation?"

"Yes. And as for how well we know each other..." She blushed a furious pink, folding all the faster. "After last night there isn't much we *don't* know about each other—except, of course, in your case, I'm still a little sketchy about your name, what you do for a living and, oh yeah, every single thing about you other than how you kiss."

"Ha! You have to admit I do that pretty damned well."

She ducked her gaze. "I will admit no such thing."

Steeling his jaw, Finn worked overtime on keeping his cool. "Excuse me, but were you in the same room as I was last night? Because if you were, I'd say you were every bit as into me as I was into you."

"How could I have been *into* you, when I don't even know you? The man I thought was my partner in the ultimate commitment two people can make is named Dallas. He's a dependable, hardworking lawyer in Salt Lake City and he loves both me and my—" She put her hand to her mouth.

"So just because you don't know me, I'm not dependable or hardworking? I'll have you know I've owned and operated my own highly successful construction business for the past ten years. I'm the very definition of dependable."

Lilly pulled the zipper around her suitcase, then stood, rewarding this Finn person's speech with a slow round of applause. "Bravo. That was very convincing.

Now, if you'd care to prove how dependable you really are, could you please take me home?''

"Sure, if you tell me where you live.''

"That's easy. As your wife, I guess I'm stuck living with you, Mr. Reilly.''

STUCK LIVING WITH HIM?

Finn cast a narrow-eyed glance across the car's front seat at his sleeping bride.

How dare she act as if being married to him was some kind of hardship? After all, a lot of the women in Greenleaf considered him to be one heck of a prize.

Right. Which must be why Vivian ran off with Mr. Motorcycle.

Fuming all the harder, Finn chose to ignore his conscience's latest sarcastic remark.

With his elbow propped on the open window, warmed by bright Utah sun, and a dry desert breeze ruffling his hair, were it not for the company of his current companion, he would have been content. Just what kind of prize did she think she was? Sitting over there snoring for the past six hours, she was about as much fun as talking to a potato.

His gaze accidentally strayed to the curve of her cute tush encased in a pair of minty-green shorts. Admittedly she was one hell of a prize in the physical department, but that was it. Other than the eye candy she provided, she was a royal pain in his—

He gripped the steering wheel harder.

Of course, yesterday, he had sort of enjoyed her company.

Sort of, my horse's behind. I couldn't get enough of

*her. I liked her laugh, and the way she looked out for
me. Tying my bow tie. Ordering my breakfast. Picking
out my clothes…kissing me like she wanted me more
than any other man in the world.*

Eyebrows furrowed, it occurred to Finn how much
he'd grown to care for Lilly over the past two days.
How many times, when he thought she'd been hired
by Mitch, had he wished things could be different between them? How many times had he longed for her
to be the woman she'd pretended to be?

Talk about being careful what you wished for.

Every single thing he'd grown to adore in Lilly was
the real deal. Even better, she was his wife.

His wife!

For years, he'd prayed to be in this very situation.

Well, not the part where his wife hated him and
thought he was the worst lowlife to ever walk the
planet, but the being-married part was still good.

He eyed Lilly again, noting the way her silky gold
curls danced in the warm breeze, tickling her cheeks,
making him green with envy that they were allowed
to touch her and he wasn't.

Dammit, this was stupid.

The fact of the matter was that, even though their
meeting was a colossal mistake, Lilly could deny it all
she wanted, but they did have chemistry. He hadn't
been with that many women, but he'd been with
enough to know that nights like the one they shared
were hardly the norm. He'd felt things with her he
hadn't even believed were possible.

Best of all, she was one hundred percent trustworthy—unlike certain other women he'd almost married.

A female who had enough moral convictions to remain married to him on a matter of principle was a hard thing to come by in this day and age. That fact alone told him that one thing he could always count on hearing from her was the truth.

Stirring beside him, she asked, "Are we almost there?"

"We've still got another forty-five minutes."

"Oh." Her tone sounded flat, as if she'd rather be scrubbing toilets than seated in a car beside him.

"You don't have to sound so excited."

"Good, because I'm not."

Finn raked his fingers through his hair. "Have you considered the fact that, aside from my name changing, I'm the same guy you were all over yesterday?"

"Ugh," she said, cradling her face in her hands. "Don't remind me. The things I revealed to you—and I'm not just talking about…" He caught her in a deep blush. "About, you know—last night—but stuff I've never told anyone but Dallas—the man I love."

"Yep, I can see where e-mailing could lead to true love."

"It did," she said, shifting on the seat to face him. "Whether you believe it or not, Dallas understood me in a way no other man ever has. He's my soul mate…" She reddened. "Well, at least he used to be."

"Which thoroughly explains why you don't want to divorce me to be with him."

Crossing her arms, she said, "You don't understand anything."

"Why don't you try explaining."

"Because after what you did, you don't deserve an

explanation.'' Lilly turned her gaze to the window, to the same unremarkable stark, brown landscape they'd been passing through for hours. Without Dallas's safety net, she might as well consider the rest of her existence as void of love as this landscape was void of life.

''I'll probably regret asking this,'' Finn said, ''but what exactly did I do that's so awful?''

''You married me under false pretenses. From the moment we first met you knew full well I had no intention of marrying you. Not even once did you question why I kept calling you Dallas.''

''I already told you, I thought somebody hired you to dupe me. And if you're wanting to play the blame game, how about accepting some of it yourself? The bar and grill you walked into is called Lu's—not Luigi's. And the second you walked up to me, you should have asked to see my ID.''

Finn looked to see how she liked them apples but soon wished he hadn't. Her big blue eyes were filling up and it'd been quite a while since the last time they had spilled. Now that he knew every tear she'd ever cried was real, he worried they'd be that much harder to take.

Before, when he thought she worked for Mitch, he'd had a good reason to harden his heart, but now, he felt kind of sorry for her—not because she'd wound up married to him, but because she was too stubborn to see him for what he was—a great catch!

''HERE WE ARE,'' Finn said while steering her car onto a winding, blacktopped driveway. ''Home sweet home.''

"Gee, don't strain yourself making me feel welcome."

"Believe me—" he flashed her a caustic smile "—after the way you've treated me today, I won't."

Ignoring him, Lilly watched three dogs that could only be described as mutts, ranging in size from a chicken to a mountain goat, tear around the side of a freestanding garage.

"Here comes the welcoming committee."

"Do they bite?"

"Nope. They might try kissing you, though." He shot a scorching wink Lilly's way before putting the car in park.

It was then she saw the house.

In a million, trillion years, she wouldn't have guessed that the stranger she'd somehow married lived in a carbon copy of her dream home. The Victorian castle was like something out of a movie. The yellow-and-white gingerbread-laced structure boasted twin turrets and even a widow's walk.

"You live here?" she said, wishing she could have erased some of her obvious awe.

"Yeah, *I* live here," he said, turning off the engine. "Why? Did you peg me for more of a shack kind of guy?"

"No, it's just that, I…" *Dreamed of living in this house my whole life—not with you, of course—but with a man who loves me.* She licked her lips and eyed the three adorable furry faces smacking their chops to get at her husband. "Let's just say you have a lovely home and leave it at that."

"Thanks," he said with the warmth of ice. Climbing out of the car, he sent the dogs into a fit of barking pleasure.

While Finn's attitude tempted her to demand he take her to her old apartment in a neighboring town, Lilly squared her shoulders and climbed out of the car, ready as she'd ever be to face her future. Hand on her tummy, she reminded herself that her whole life she'd been getting into bad spots and either covering them up or running away, but this time, this problem, she'd face dead on. Over the years, she'd put her parents through a lot of trauma, but this disaster took the cake. If they discovered she'd virtually hired a husband, only to end up not marrying him but a stranger, she wouldn't blame them for washing their hands of her.

"Ready to head inside?"

"Sure." As the biggest of the mutts, what looked to be an odd cross between a sheep dog and a dachshund, approached for a cautious sniff, she patted him between his ears. "What's his name?"

"Moe. The middle-sized beagle mix is Larry, and the oversize Yorkie-terrier is Curly Sue."

"Nice to meet you all" she said, giving Larry and Curly Sue pats, too. As much as she tried holding her anger toward Finn intact, she'd always loved dogs and knew that any man who'd take in three such downright goofy looking beasts couldn't be all bad.

She gestured toward the trunk. "Shouldn't we carry in the luggage?"

"Leave it," he growled. "I'll get it later."

On a meandering brick path, she fell into step beside him. "Any time now, feel free to thaw your arctic chill. I mean, I wasn't the one who doctored *my* marriage license by adding *your* name."

"Thanks," Finn said. "I'm feeling so much better now that you've pointed that out."

"You're welcome. I'm just doing my part to keep you on the straight and narrow."

"Oh, that's ripe coming from you, Miss Misfit."

"Yeah," she said, edging past him on the path, "but thanks to you, my correct title would now be, *Mrs.* Misfit." Eyeing the grand home up close, Lilly froze. "Not that you should take this as any reflection as to the way I feel about you, but again—wow. Nice house."

"Thanks, again. I think." Had she only imagined his voice softening?

"Did you build it?"

"Nah, the house is over a hundred years old, but I did restore it to its original grandeur. It's been in my family for all that time, but..." Finn couldn't bring himself to tell her that when his mom, dad and sister had died, he'd had to abandon this special place to live with his aunt in her mountain home located roughly forty-five minutes west of Greenleaf. The house was uncared-for through the years it took him to turn eighteen, and by the time he moved back in, he'd practically had to gut the entire structure.

Climbing the stairs leading to the wraparound porch, his feeling of pride choked him up. Eight white wicker rockers sat amongst red-impatience-topped side tables. That was one oversize rocker for him, one for his wife, and six for their kids. Leafy ferns hung from each of the porch's arches, drinking in what was left of the unseasonably warm Indian summer day.

Though you couldn't have paid him to admit it, he liked the way his bride stood gaping.

"This place is incredible," she said. "I can't get over how neat and tidy everything is. When my brothers were bachelors, their houses were always wrecks."

"What can I say? I run a tight ship."

"Can we go inside?"

"Might as well." He reached for her legs, but she squealed and backed away.

"What are you doing?" she demanded.

"Carrying you over the threshold. That's what newlyweds are supposed to do, isn't it?"

"Normal newlyweds, but we're hardly that."

Sighing, he crossed his arms over his chest. "So let me get this straight. because you don't believe in divorce after a couple sleep together, that means we're stuck with each other for the next fifty or so years, right?"

"Y-yes."

"And in all those fifty years, you plan on wielding this cold shoulder of yours as weapon?"

"I didn't say that. All I said was that I'd prefer you not carry me over the threshold. It's such a romantic, old-fashioned custom that if we were to take part in it, I'd feel guilty."

"Even though we'd have seven years of bad luck if we don't do it?"

"That's if you break a mirror. I don't think the

threshold thing carries any cosmic punishment if you don't follow it, do you?''

"Beats the heck out of me, but at least I got you to think about something other than how awful I am." He thought he spied a glimmer of a smile behind her shadowed eyes and touched his index finger to the corner of her mouth. "I'm not making you laugh, am I?"

"No."

"Then how come that dimple in your left cheek is almost showing."

"I don't have a dimple," she said, grinning all the more.

"You do, too. During Sparky's big clown routine, I saw that dimple peeking quite a few times."

"Okay, okay," she said, now fully laughing. "I admit it, I have a dimple, but I got sick of my brothers teasing me about having a hole in my face, so don't you tease me, too."

He made grave business of marking an X across his chest. "Cross my heart and hope to—"

"Leave that last part off," she said. "I never like to hear people casually mention dying."

"Should I take that as a positive sign that at least you don't want me to croak?"

"Ha-ha."

"Wow, was that two laughs in a row from Miss Uptight?"

"Remember? All put-downs should now be in the form of a *Mrs*. And no, that wasn't a laugh, but sarcasm—there is a difference."

"Great. Now that we've cleared that up, how about

it?'' He lunged for her legs. ''Will you let me carry you over the threshold?''

Something deep inside Lilly longed to say yes, but the practical side of her said, ''No. I just wouldn't feel right.'' The minute she saw the crestfallen expression on Finn's face, she regretted turning him down, but then why should she care about his feelings when he'd so callously played with hers?

This whole mess could have been easily avoided if only he'd admitted not knowing her from the start, but now... Now she wasn't sure what to do, other than get through life minute by minute and try to string those minutes into some semblance of normalcy.

The playful spirit that had been present only a few minutes earlier had been replaced by a chilly north wind that had nothing to do with the day's sunshine and everything to do with her new husband.

Turning from her, he placed his key in the door's lock and turned it. With a lonely creak, the door swung open and he stepped aside. ''After you.''

''Thanks.'' Before her eyes even had a chance to adjust to the interior's gloom, she heard Finn stomp down the porch stairs. ''Are you getting the luggage?'' she called out. ''Want me to help?''

''Nope. I'll get it later.'' He headed across the velvety green lawn—not toward the car.

''Where are you going?''

''Doesn't matter,'' he shouted without slowing or looking back. ''Make yourself at home.''

Home. Despite the day's heat, she rubbed her suddenly chilled forearms. Why was it that the beautiful house didn't seem nearly as welcoming without Finn?

Chapter Seven

"Finn!" Lu called out the minute he stepped up to the bar. "It's good to see you. None the worse for wear, I suppose?"

"I wish." The beer-cryin' music playing over the jukebox hardly lightened his mood.

"Ah now, what's got you down? Did that cupcake you left here with get some sense in her head and decide not to marry you?"

All he could do was laugh, for if he didn't laugh over his ever-worsening situation with Lilly, he'd end up crying, and he was much too manly to indulge in tears.

Lu set a long-neck beer in front of him before wiping her hands on the tea towel she kept hanging behind the bar. "Don't look so glum. Surely Mitch isn't really going to take Abigail, and even if he does, at least that pretty little bride didn't run off with your heart. That's the prospect that had me worried—that and the fact that you'd be off the market to a gal who'd truly love you the way you deserve to be loved."

"Sorry to disappoint you, Lu, but you're wrong on every account. Care to join me in a toast?" He raised his beer to the few other folks at the bar. Old drunken Pete was sawing logs at his usual spot, and since Finn figured the old guy needed his beauty sleep far more than he needed another drink, he didn't bother waking him.

Lu's eyes narrowed to slits. "What is it we're toasting?"

"What else? My new bride."

"Congratulations," said a long-haired fellow Finn didn't recognize from a few stools down. His girl echoed those sentiments before they both raised their brown bottles to him and his wife.

Far from being happy about his news, Lu scowled. "Please tell me this is a joke. You didn't really marry that girl, did you?"

"Oh, yeah. I sure as hell did."

"Oh, Finn. Have your aunt and I taught you nothing over the years?"

"Guess not," he said, after taking another sip of beer.

"Good gracious gravy," the bartender said to no one in particular. "If this don't beat all. So? Where is she?"

"At the house."

"Her house, or yours?"

"Mine."

"And how do you feel about finally havin' a woman in that shrine to a future family you call home?"

He shrugged, took another sip of beer. "I could be better."

Elbows on the bar, she asked, "Feel like talkin' about it?"

He shook his head. "I'd rather drink about it."

"Don't you mean think?"

"Nope. I'm thinking clearer than ever, and I definitely meant *drink*."

Lu made a clucking sound. "Aw, now, Finn, you don't really mean that."

"What doesn't pretty boy here mean?"

Finn groaned.

Mitch. Just the guy he *didn't* want to see.

"You ready to hand over my money?" Mitch said, heaving himself onto the stool beside Finn.

"Sorry, old pal, but you lose."

"The hell you say. It's only Monday. What woman in her right mind would up and marry you after only knowin' you a day?"

"Her name's Lilly," Lu said, setting a draft beer in front of Mitch. "Pretty little thing, too. Saw her myself Saturday night—not an hour after your own girl practically had to wheelbarrow your drunken behind outta here."

The big man snarled. "I don't believe it. Show me proof."

Finn reached for his wallet and drew out the marriage license that had him in such hot water with Lilly. Showing the license to Mitch should have been a defining moment of his life, so how come it felt flat?

After a few minutes of careful reading, Mitch slammed his fist on the bar, rattling everyone's beers and Lu's few fancy wineglasses. "Damn you, Reilly. I know this is a trick."

At that, Finn laughed. "Trust me, old pal, the only trick here is being played on me. I'm the one stuck with a wife who's gonna hate me for the rest of my life."

THE KITCHEN CLOCK STARTED to chime in exact harmony with the hall grandfather clock. When the duo reached ten, Lilly, lingering over a pot of peppermint tea at the oak kitchen table, sighed, trying not to let the quiet in the rambling old house consume her.

Where was her husband?

Had her not allowing him to carry her over the threshold hurt his feelings that badly? She hadn't meant anything personal by it. It was just that her whole life she'd dreamed of partaking in the quaint old custom, only a big part of that dream had been making it come true with a man she loved.

Yes, Finn Reilly had been perfectly pleasant to her over the past two days, but that didn't bring her any closer to even liking him, let alone loving him. Without a trace of conscience, he'd tricked her into marrying him. And now, because of her own overblown conscience—not to mention fear of being caught in yet another disastrous mess—she was legally and morally bound to him forever. Which, considering how nice his house was, shouldn't have been that bad, but somehow the realization didn't make her feel any better.

The kitchen was a cook's dream with its stainless steel fridge and stove that boasted four gas burners and a grill that would be perfect for Saturday morning burgers. The countertops were made of cobalt-blue tiles and the backsplashes had contrasting yellow-and-white tiles with blue flowers. All the cupboards were incredibly well stocked with not only food but dishes, china and flatware—all services for eight.

Upstairs, there were even sleeping spaces for eight—ten counting the sunny guest room where she'd unpacked her belongings. The king-size master bed could have slept four, but every time she even thought about sharing the bed with Finn, her insides turned to mush.

That morning, when he asked her what kind of a kisser she thought he was, she'd lied when she told him he wasn't all that great. And maybe what they'd done in the big fur-piled bed in Vegas was partially what had her so upset. All her life, she'd tried so hard to be prim and proper—the kind of daughter her parents would be proud of—but how could a proper woman do what she'd done with a man she didn't even know?

But I do know him. He's my husband.

Ugh, he might have technically been her husband, but seeing how she hadn't even known his real name at the time she'd slept with him, somehow that made their magical night seem soiled. She wanted so badly to fit in with the wholesome, perfect, overachieving image the rest of her family portrayed, but yet again, she was the square peg trying to squeeze into a round hole.

She was the one who'd set fire to the family kitchen by leaving Jiffy Pop sizzling on the stove to answer a much-awaited call from Phil, her high school boyfriend. She was the one who'd lost jobs as both a grocery store clerk and a bank teller because she kept forgetting to set her morning wake-up alarm. Worst of all, she was the one who'd believed Elliot when he told her he loved her and would marry her and then, only *after* she slept with him, had he told her he was already married.

By now, the cumulative pain of a lifetime spent messing up had taken its toll and Lilly started to cry. She'd never flat out bawled as much as she had the past two days.

Was this normal?

Was she normal?

Was her baby normal?

The more she fretted the more she cried, and when the back door opened and Finn came rushing in, asking "Lilly, honey, what's wrong?" It only seemed natural to stand up and go running into his arms. "I've ruined everything," she sobbed against his chest. "I've ruined your life and mine and—"

"Shh," he said, smoothing her hair. "You haven't ruined anything. In fact, in marrying me, you did an extraordinarily, extra superspecial thing."

After drying her eyes on his red T-shirt, which smelled faintly of cigarette smoke and beer, she sniffled, then asked, "What?"

"By marrying me, you won the bet. Look, Mitch paid me a thousand bucks cash." He fished a wad of ten hundred-dollar bills from the back pocket of his jeans and handed it to her. "If it'll cheer you up, this is all yours."

"I don't want that money. It's tainted, just like our marriage."

Finn frowned. "That's what Lu said you'd say, but I figured you to be a whole lot smarter than that."

"Oh?" She raised the golden arches she called eyebrows. Funny, but in the time he'd been at Lu's, Finn had forgotten how pretty his wife was. Pretty as the sunrise on that calendar his accountant gave him every year for Christmas.

"Have you been drinking?" she asked, hands on her saucy hips.

"Not that much."

"Uh-huh, and how did you get home?"

"I brought him." Matt strolled through the back door. "Figured he wasn't fit to drive."

"And you would be?" Lilly asked.

"I'm his best friend. Matthew Marshall at your service, ma'am. I was outside putting those mangy mutts to bed in the barn." He removed a green Greenleaf Lumber ball cap before reaching forward to shake her hand. "Finn and I here have been through everything together. I thought it was only right that I meet his bride as soon as I had the chance."

"Thank you for driving him home, Matthew. I'm Lilly Churchill—or I guess that's Lilly Reilly now, huh?"

"And what a sweet name it is," Finn said, resting his head on his wife's shoulder. He gazed at the ceiling. "Yo, Matt-o, when did I install a rotating chandelier over this table?"

"You didn't, bud, which is why it's probably a good idea if I get you up to bed." Though Matt was a few inches shorter than his friend, he put Finn's right arm over his shoulder and guided him toward the stairs.

"Do you need help?" Lilly asked, trailing after them.

"Nah, I should be able to handle him. My buddy here never drinks more than he can handle unless he's upset over a woman—and even then he's only been this drunk three times in his life."

"When was that?" Lilly couldn't keep from asking.

"Well, let me think. One, would have to be the day Linda, his old high school flame, left Greenleaf to go to some fancy college out east. Two, would be last Saturday night when he was so upset over Vivian doing what she did. And three, well, that's right now."

"Aw, now, don't go tellin' her all my secrets," Finn protested midway up the stairs.

"I didn't tell all of them," Matt said, casting Lilly a wink. "Just the ones I knew you'd be most embarrassed about."

A FEW MINUTES AFTER Matt had left and Finn had fallen asleep spread-eagled in the center of his king-size bed, Lilly removed her husband's work boots and covered him with a wedding-ring quilt.

The room's forest-green walls were soothing, and sitting in a corner rocker, immersed in only the yellow glow of a bedside lamp, Lilly closed her eyes, breathing deeply of the lemon oil Finn must have rubbed into the antique dressers.

From outside came the faint sound of a few hardy crickets. Inside, all was quiet save for the creaking of her chair rails against the hardwood floor and the sound of Finn's fitful snoring.

She opened her eyes to gaze upon his sleeping face. Finn. Her husband. The man who would hopefully be a good father to her baby. Despite the fact that he was sleeping, his expression was weary, as if life had dealt him far more than he could comfortably handle.

Abruptly she stopped rocking and went to him, perching beside him. Tentatively she touched his face, traced the fine lines around his eyes and mouth. Did those lines mean he'd led a hard life? Or were they laugh lines earned by more happiness than sorrow?

Could what his friend said be true? That Finn had been this drunk only two other times in his life and both those times had been over a woman?

Vivian. That was his fiancée, who'd run out on their wedding. Her lips turning up in a melancholy smile, Lilly couldn't say she blamed Finn for turning to beer to soothe that kind of pain. His wedding day must have been humiliating. So humiliating in fact, that in retrospect, she could almost understand the rationale behind his taking this Mitch character up on his bet.

Okay, so she understood Finn's bet, but that didn't mean she liked it. And that understanding did nothing to answer one more question she couldn't get out of her head. The question of how he felt about her. For if she'd been the third woman who'd driven Finn to drink, had he been drinking because now that she was in his life, he wanted her out? Or because she was out of his life and he wanted her in?

FINN WOKE to merciless sun spearing his eyes. The scent of frying hamburger ambushed his nose. With his gut in a too-much-beer uproar, he couldn't tell if the meat smelled bad or good. And for that matter, who in the hell was cooking it? He lived alone.

"'I'm gonna wash that man right out of my hair, I'm gonna wash that man right out of my hair, I'm gonna wash that man right out of my hair, and send him on his waaaaay!'"

Correction—he *used* to live alone.

From the sounds and smells of it, his bride was in the kitchen cooking breakfast.

Washing his face with his hands, he groaned.

His mother used to sing while she cooked. Finding a woman who sang had always been at the top of Finn's must-have list for a wife. Hearing Lilly belting out a show tune only made him wonder that much more if maybe they could make a go of their marriage. If Lilly would just forget about his bet and start thinking about the real him.

Sometime during the night, he'd dreamed she was beside him. He'd even slipped his arm around her waist to hold her tight. Then that dream had turned nightmare when she'd left. For a brief time, his life-long goal of filling his home with a new family had been poised on the brink of coming true, but now, he wasn't sure what to think.

Even if Lilly wanted kids, that didn't mean she'd ever again let him close enough to make any!

Footsteps sounded on the stairs and for a minute he was so confused about seeing her that he almost feigned sleep. But it was too late for that now.

She stood in the open door, hands on her hips, lips pressed into a tight frown. "You're up."

"Barely."

"Do you know it's after eleven?"

"It's my honeymoon," he fired back with a half-hearted grin. "What's the harm in a man sleeping late?"

"None, I suppose." Her expression softened and he detected a glint of a smile in her eyes. "I came up to tell you that if you're hungry, breakfast is ready."

"Thanks." He rolled onto his side. "You didn't have to cook anything, you know."

"I know, but seeing as how I was starved, I figured I might as well fix extra for you."

"Gee, that's the nicest thing you've done for me since you found out who I really am. This doesn't mean I'm starting to grow on you, does it?"

"No." Even as she said the word, Lilly couldn't help but remember where she had awakened, spooned against her husband with his arm snug around her waist. During her first few minutes of consciousness, she'd felt indescribably content, then she remembered this wasn't kind and compassionate Dallas she was cozied up to, but a man who'd tricked her into marriage.

So, Lilly Reilly, if you're so all-fired certain Dallas Lebeaux is the true man for you, why not go to him? Explain everything? Surely, he'd understand? He'd have you out of this house and away from this stranger who makes your pulse race, faster than you can say Oops, I messed up again.

Lilly swallowed hard and raised her chin a barely

perceptible notch. No. That had been the old Lilly thinking. For the new and improved Lilly, running away wasn't even an option. Nope, for the baby, and most importantly, for herself, no more running from her problems. The new Lilly faced them head-on.

The soulful look her square-jawed, whisker-stubbled, dark-eyed god of a husband currently graced her with should have made her feel better about that decision, but all it really did was serve as a flustering reminder of their long, hot Vegas night.

He cleared his throat. "About last night," he said. "I never meant to come home in that condition."

"It's all right." Toying with one of her curls, she added, "These things happen."

"Not to me, they don't. Like I told you Sunday morning, I'm not a drinking man."

"Yet this is the second time I've seen you drunk. Sorry," she said. "I didn't mean that to sound so harpy. I guess it's none of my business what you do."

"The hell it isn't. You're my wife, and if you're so all-fired determined for us to stay married, then we might as well start acting like we're married, don't you think?"

She shot her gaze out the window, glad he wasn't in on her secret that, very much like a wife, she'd fallen asleep beside him and stayed with him all night.

"Lilly?"

"I'm sorry," she said, already on her way out of the room with her hands cupping her tummy. "I can't deal with this right now. You. Us. It's all too much."

Ignoring the pounding in his head, Finn went to her, grasping her by the shoulders and gently urging her around. "If not now, when are you going to deal with this, Lilly? Obviously, as we both saw last night, I'm not dealing with our sudden union too well, either. I'm not saying that me knocking back one too many beers was your fault, because it wasn't. What I am saying is that maybe we ought to spend some time together over the next few days. You know, getting to know each other. Talking about our childhoods."

"How is talking about what we did as kids going to make me trust you? Don't you see? I entered this marriage believing you were one man and you turned out to be another. How will I ever know if what we share is real, or another one of your games?"

Releasing her, Finn let out a harsh sigh. "For the last time, Lilly, I never would have gone through with our wedding if I hadn't believed you were every bit as determined to dupe me as I was you. My whole life I've wanted to be—" He looked her way to see that, instead of focusing on him, her attention was aimed somewhere around their feet. "Never mind," he said, heading for the shower. "I can see you could care less about anything I have to say."

"Finn, I—"

It was too late for apologies. He'd already slammed the bathroom door.

Chapter Eight

"I don't know," Matt said late that afternoon while he and Finn went over the latest changes to Mrs. Kleghorn's master bath. "I thought she seemed nice— not to mention hot, in a June Cleaveresque sort of way."

"You talking about Mrs. Kleghorn or my wife?"

"That's pretty funny," Matt said, delivering a sucker punch to Finn's left arm. "Even hungover, you're a stand-up kind of guy."

"I'm not hungover," Finn growled, using his red pen to savagely scratch out the lines on the blueprint showing where his client wanted her bathroom fridge. "And who the hell ever heard of putting a minibar in a bathroom?"

"You can't blame her for being upset with you, bud. After all, finding out you've been the butt of a joke would be tough for anyone to take, let alone a sensitive woman like Lilly."

Finn counted to four and a half before he blew. "You think she's so great, why don't you marry her? Now, if you don't mind, could we please get some work done? If this fridge is going to be in the bath, we're going to have to reroute all of Arnold's wiring through the master closet.'' He pointed to the spot on the plans.

"If I were you," Matt said, leaning against a framed-out window, staring at the mountain view, "I'd woo her."

"*Woo* her? Mrs. Kleghorn doesn't need wooing, just a dose of reality." He rolled up the plans and slapped the paper tube against Matt's gut. "See that Arnold gets these changes. I've got a meeting with the motel folks."

"Can you say please?"

"Watch it," Finn warned, already on the way to his truck.

"Hey," Matt shouted. "I thought you were taking this week off?"

"I was. Then a woman named Lilly moved into my house and now I never want to go home again."

"Cool. Does that mean we're still on for Friday night poker?"

LILLY PICKED UP the kitchen phone, took a deep breath and managed to punch in a whole three numbers before she chickened out and pressed the disconnect doohickey.

"Come on, Churchill—I mean, Reilly," she coached. "You're never going to get a grip on your future if you don't at least try tackling the past." Calling Dallas had to be done.

Later.

Marching to the side-by-side fridge, she opened the freezer section and happily discovered a stash of goodies. Super Duper Commando Trooper Popsicles, Drumsticks, Minnie Mouse shaped ice-cream sandwiches and even a half gallon of Rocky Road. Selecting a Drumstick, she unwrapped it, then went to work gobbling all the chopped nuts and chocolate from the top.

Midway into the cone section of her snack, she wondered what in the world a manly contractor was doing with a bunch of kiddy treats in his freezer. She could see a guy enjoying a bowl of Rocky Road after dinner, but a Commando Trooper Pop?

She tossed her wrapper into the trash can tucked beneath the sink.

"You can do this," she said, once again picking up the phone. "Dallas deserves to know the truth."

Yeah, and my stomach deserves some peace.

Confrontations had never been her strong point and while she didn't think for a second Dallas would be rude, the mystery of not knowing how he would react was starting to get to her.

"Okay, you big chicken," she said, taking one more fortifying breath. "You've had chocolate. You've had ice cream. It's do or die. Crunch time."

After punching the numbers to Dallas's office in real fast, she closed her eyes, halfheartedly praying his secretary wouldn't pick up. Unfortunately, she did, and seconds later, the woman patched her through.

"Lilly," Dallas's rich voice was laced with concern. "What happened to you? I've been worried sick."

"I'm sorry," she said, twisting the phone cord around her pinkie. "Some things kind of happened."

"What kind of *things?*" Was that a pencil she heard tapping in the background? "You haven't fallen ill, have you? Is your baby all right?"

"The baby and I are fine, but I've run into a bit of a snafu where our, um…engagement is concerned."

"Oh?"

"Yeah, you see, I'm, ah…kind of, sort of already married."

For a long time, there was just silence, then a chuckle. "This is a joke, right?"

"Um, no." She drew her lower lip into her mouth for a quick nibble.

"Lilly, I'm in line for partnership—a partnership that hinges upon my having a wife. I've told the entire firm all about you. How we had this whirlwind Miami fling, and now—"

"We never went to Miami!"

"I know, but my bosses don't have to know that. Besides, I was just laying a little foundation work for when I told them about the baby."

"Oh."

He sighed. "You've ruined my life and all you can say is 'oh'?"

Hot tears pooled. While she told him the details about what had happened, Lilly blinked to fight back the tears. "I'm sorry, it's not as if I married the wrong guy on purpose. I mean, your directions to Luigi's were awful, and it was dark, and I've never been good at finding my way at night."

"Lady," he said in a cruel tone, "from where I'm sitting, you're apparently not good at anything. Good riddance."

Hands trembling, Lilly carefully hung the phone back in its cradle. Dallas's words hurt. The old Lilly would have sought comfort by telling herself what he said wasn't true, but deep down, she feared it was. Was she kidding herself with all this hyped-up talk of starting over and facing her problems head-on? Was such a transformation even possible?

One tear fell, and then another and another, until they were coming so fast Lilly could hardly see. In the back of her mind, she'd used the idea of running back to Dallas as a sort of safety net, but now that net was gone. Even worse, she was married to a man who couldn't stand the sight of her.

Boy, she thought with a hiccuping sigh. Being responsible sure wasn't fun.

IT WAS PUSHING SIX by the time Finn finished with the owners of the motel he'd be constructing by the highway. The Good-night Inn would be pretty much a run-of-the-mill roadside place. No frills, with the exception of an indoor pool, which, considering how tight his neck was at the thought of seeing Lilly again, would have been damn nice to jump into.

Pulling into the driveway of his house, he did his usual double horn-honk and by the time he parked Abigail beside Lilly's sedan, two dark-headed kids and all three dogs had come running through the miniforest of firs dividing the neighbor's yard from his.

"Finn! I mithed you!" said Chrissy, the youngest, with a huge grin as he stepped out of the truck. She'd lost both front teeth the previous week and hadn't quite gotten the hang of speaking without them yet.

When she gave him a fierce hug, his heart swelled with affection for the runt.

Her nine-year-old brother, Randy, who everybody called Rambo because of his affinity for anything to do with the hot new line of toys called Super Duper Commando Troopers, was quick to follow with a hug of his own. "Mom said Miss Lu told her you already got married again," he said. "But I thought Vivian rode off with that motorcycle guy at the wedding?"

"Randy," Chrissy scolded. "Mommy said Finn's senthative about motorcycles."

"Not motorcycles, you dork. Girls."

"I'm a girl."

"You're a dork."

"Whoa," Finn said, stepping in to referee while ushering the two through the tail-wagging dogs and around the side of the house to the back door. "Your sister's a princess, Rambo, not a dork."

"Ew, gross…" Randy made a face that looked like he'd swallowed a spoonful of maggots. "She's a princess all right, Princess Dork."

"Finn? Did you hear what he thaid? That ithn't nithe."

"Come on, gang," Finn said on the back porch steps. "Let's call a truce, okay? Rambo, your mom's right, I did get married, not to Vivian, but to a woman named Lilly." *Who hates my guts, but hopefully she'll be perfectly pleasant to you little beasties.*

"Ith she pretty?" Chrissy asked, melting him with her big brown eyes.

"Very. Now, I mean it, you two. Be nice."

"Do you kiss her?" Randy asked as they stepped through the door.

As luck would have it, Finn's bride was sitting at the table reading a book that she quickly shut then shoved beneath a pile of glossy magazines. "You're home," she said. "And you brought company." Pushing back her chair, she stood to crouch before the kids. "Hi, I'm Lilly."

"You *are* pretty," Chrissy said. "Finn thaid you were and he callth me a printheth and I think you're a printheth, too. Oh—and my name's Chrithy."

"It's nice to meet you," Lilly said, solemnly shaking the girl's hand. She took a quick peek at her husband to find him glancing toward a ceiling vent.

"Is your hair color real?" Randy asked. "My aunt dyes her hair blond and wears *reeeaaallly* long fake fingernails. My dad says she looks like a—"

"This is my good friend, Randy," Finn said, saving them all the embarrassment of hearing Rambo's dad's assessment of his sister-in-law.

Grinning, Lilly said, "Yep, my hair is real and so are my nails." She held them out for inspection.

"Cool," the boy said. "Did you remember our surprise?" he asked Finn.

"Yep, you both have a treat waiting for you in the freezer."

"Awesome." He was already racing across the room with Chrissy close on his heals.

Lilly said, "I wondered who the Commando Pops and Minnie Mouse bars were for. Somehow, Finn, you didn't strike me as the Minnie type."

"Gee, thanks," he said with a grimace. "I think. Hey, what smells so good?"

"I hope you like broccoli, chicken and cheese casserole. Not knowing what time you'd be home, I thought that and a salad would be the safest choice for dinner. It'll be ready in about—" she eyed the small clock built into the oven control panel "—twenty minutes."

"That sounds delicious. Thanks."

"You're welcome."

"Chrissy threw her wrapper on the floor!"

"Did not! It wath an accident!"

"Liar!"

"You're a liar—and Mommy thaid don't call me that!"

"Takes one to know one."

"Aren't they charming?" Finn said to Lilly before breaking up yet another squabble. "Come on, kids," he said, shepherding them to the back door. "I think I hear your mother calling."

"No she isn't," Randy said. "She's busy watchin' *Young and the Restless*. She had to tape it today because my aunt's car's busted and she needed a ride to the auto shop. Dad says that bum she's dating burned up the transmiss—"

"Man, would you look at the time," Finn said, nudging them out the door. "I'll see you again tomorrow."

Chrissy gave him a fierce hug. "Bye, Finn. I love you."

Kissing the top of her head, he said, "I love you, too."

"Bye, Finn." Randy was also quick with a hug, but instead of kissing him, Finn gave him a noogie. Lord, he loved these two. They could be a real pain in the neck sometimes, but he didn't know what he'd do without them. If he felt this connected to the neighbor kids, he couldn't even imagine the joy having his own son or daughter would bring.

The second the kids left, awkward silence crept in like a third person in the room.

Finn was almost ready to call Randy and Chrissy back when Lilly said, "I, um, guess I'll set the table."

"Why don't you let me?"

"That's okay. I'm sure you'd like to wash up before we eat. Anyway, I feel kind of antsy after staying home all day. I'm usually just now getting home from work myself."

"What do you do?" Finn asked, heading for the sink to wash his hands.

"I'm a bookstore clerk. At least I used to be." Lilly took a bowl of already mixed and washed greens from the fridge. "Last Friday was my last day. Dallas is part of a big law firm in Salt Lake City. Once we were married, I planned to stay home and do the housewife thing."

"Aren't you going to miss your work?" Finn asked above the running water.

I do now, but I'm sure I won't once the baby comes.

"I'd go nuts sitting around the house all day."

"It has been a pretty strange day, but not so much because I couldn't find anything to do, but because of the way you left this morning."

Drying his hands on a cobalt-blue tea towel, he said,

"I meant what I said this morning, about us needing to spend time together."

Her back to him, she set the salad bowl on the table. "I know."

He stepped behind her, softly cupping his hands over her shoulders. To keep from leaning deeper into his touch, she tensed. Why, when her head knew Finn thought so little of her feelings that he'd used her as the object of a bet, did her body trill just being near him?

"Do you know, Lilly? Or are you just paying me lip service? Telling me what I want to hear?" He gently spun her to face him and tucked his fingers beneath her chin, urging her to meet his gaze.

Her heart pounded and her breathing stalled.

"Because if that is what you're doing, it needs to stop. I can't be in a relationship with a woman who won't even look me in the eyes. I deserve more than that and so do you."

She nodded.

"I've been a bear all day to everyone I work with. And about thirty minutes ago, I even gave Mitch, my biggest competitor and worst enemy, his cash—the cash I won because I married you. Don't you see? I'm trying to make up for my mistakes, Lilly. Can't you at least try to forgive me for making them?"

Again, all she could do was nod, because her throat had grown too tight to speak.

The oven timer went off and she sagged with relief at the intrusion.

"Can't that wait?" Finn asked.

"No," she said, already reaching for hot pads. "Dry casserole is the worst."

A sad chuckle fell from his lips as he muttered, "Dry casserole doesn't sound half as miserable as fifty years worth of dry marriage."

LATE THAT NIGHT, long after their silent meal and an endless succession of watching meaningless sitcoms, Lilly had gone to bed in the guest room and Finn let her.

Truth be told, he thought, roaming the big house, locking up and turning off lights, he'd been relieved to see her go. Trying to keep his mood on an even keel around her was a lot like dealing with Mrs. Kleghorn.

In other words...impossible!

For the life of him, Finn couldn't figure out why Lilly even wanted to stay married to him. Was she a masochist? Because even though his whole life he'd dreamed of marrying and raising a family, he'd never wanted a marriage on these terms.

His gut, remembering how right things had felt between them in Vegas, told Finn to take it slow with Lilly and she'd eventually come around. But his heart told him that logic was flawed. What they had shared in Vegas hadn't been real, but an illusion. The reason Lilly had come across as so relaxed and comfortable with him was because she thought he was that Dallas guy. Now she realized that being married to Finn was the equivalent of being told she had to suffer through a fifty-year blind date!

Yeah, buddy, and that was some kind of suffering *you two did Sunday night.*

Finn cursed under his breath.

He was about to flick off the light over the kitchen table when a pile of magazines on the floor beside the chair Lilly had sat in caught his eye. He remembered her putting those magazines over a book she'd been reading when he walked in with the neighbor kids. Curiosity had him kneeling to scoop up the whole pile and set it on the table.

The magazines were all fairly standard stuff. Vivian's past issues of *People, Cosmo,* and *National Enquirer.* The book on the other hand, was a dog-eared copy of *What to Expect When You're Expecting.*

Wondering if his bride could be pregnant, Finn's heart nearly surged out of his chest, then he remembered the crazy night Matt's sister had gone into labor.

They'd all been playing poker around the kitchen table when Rachel's water broke. Her entire pregnancy, she'd carried that book with her everywhere, consulting it as if it were her pregnancy bible. In all the excitement over getting her to the hospital, she forgot the book and once the baby arrived, she switched from *What to Expect When You're Expecting* to a thick tome on baby psychology and feeding habits.

But Lilly wasn't pregnant. She must have just been bored. Since Finn haphazardly stacked reading material into the big wicker basket his aunt gave him for laundry, he figured his wife had come across the book there.

Kicking himself for being such a hopeless dreamer

when it came to the topic of starting a family, Finn flicked off the kitchen light.

Only in the shadowy moonlight could he find the courage to admit how much all of this hurt. Here he was, finally married, and not only was his wife sleeping in the guest room, but when he tried starting a conversation, she wouldn't say more than five words.

Hell, he thought, walking by rote through the darkened front hall, then climbing the stairs. He of all people knew their relationship had been built on a foundation of sand, but he was a contractor specializing in renovations. He'd asked her if she wanted to spend this week getting to know each other all over again, but she'd turned him down flat.

Beyond Lilly's great looks and bod, he was as intrigued as hell by her morals and mind. Unlike Vivian, Lilly—aside from the fact that she despised him—was Finn's ideal. Loyal, intelligent, trustworthy, dependable—she even sang while she cooked. She'd make a great mom, would never keep secrets, and best of all, she'd never, ever lie. He'd once thought all of that of Vivian, but look how she'd proved him wrong. Now, with Lilly, just by the way she'd reacted to the news of his bet, he knew beyond a shadow of a doubt that she was as genuine as a woman could get.

At the top of the stairs, he flicked on the dim hall light and eyed the closed door to her room.

What did the woman want from him? A bended-knee apology along with chocolate and a few dozen roses?

If I were you, I'd woo her.

From out of nowhere, Matt's suggestion appeared like a beacon in the night.

Was that it? Could the solution to his dilemma be that simple? Was romancing Lilly the key to transforming her into a real wife?

WHEN LILLY WOKE the next morning to another brilliant fall day, she frowned. Why was it, when her mood felt edgy as an approaching storm, the weather refused to cooperate?

Squeezing her eyes shut, she tried falling back asleep, but it was no use. She was wide-awake and, judging by the sound of the shower being turned off across the hall, her husband was awake, too.

Was today the day to tell him about her baby?

He'd seemed fine about the neighbor kids traipsing through the house, and the fact that he even bought them special treats told her he wasn't a complete ogre when it came to the subject of children. And talk about a character witness—when Chrissy gave Finn that hug and told him she loved him…

Ugh, just thinking about how sweet the moment had been made Lilly's eyes well with tears.

Okay, so at the moment, all signs were positive that Finn, unlike Elliot, the baby's real father, would make a great dad—assuming she gathered the courage to tell him.

She sat up only to have a wave of nausea hit like a tsunami.

Hand over her mouth, she raced to the end of the hall, wishing the whole way that when she'd chosen a bedroom, she'd picked one with an adjoining bath.

Just in time, she made it to the porcelain throne.

At the sink, holding a wet washcloth to her head, she glanced in the mirror. The face staring back looked tinted a shade between gruel and wallpaper paste.

Speaking of wallpaper…the burgundy-and-gold paisley pattern on the wall behind her was doing nothing to calm her already frazzled nerves.

A knock sounded on the door. "Lilly? You all right?"

Looking to the ceiling, she sent up a one-word prayer.

Why?

"Um, yeah," she said, holding the cloth to her forehead. "I'm fine."

"You don't sound fine. Can I come in?"

"No."

"Why not? You sounded pretty sick. Maybe I can help."

Help? Not unless he knew of a magical method to get her into her second trimester. The pregnancy book she'd been reading said that was typically when morning sickness let up.

Earlier in her pregnancy she'd experienced a bout of the dreaded malaise, but nothing like this. In fact, maybe this wasn't morning sickness at all but flu?

"Lilly? I'm not leaving until either you come out or let me in."

Glancing one more time at her ghoulish reflection, Lilly opened the door. "There, now that you've verified I'm still alive, will you leave?"

"Wow, you really are sick. You look awful."

"Thanks."

"Sorry," he said, shoving his hands into the pockets of his faded jeans. His broad chest was encased in a mossy green T-shirt that did amazing things to his soulful brown eyes, and his hair was still damp from the shower. In short, he looked disgustingly handsome and she looked worse than death! "I didn't mean to ruffle your womanly feathers," he added. "Just making an observation."

"Yeah, well, next time you feel like observing, keep your comments to yourself." Holding tight to her few remaining shreds of dignity, she tugged the hem of her brother Mark's red football jersey as low as it would go, then shuffled past Finn, ignoring the numbness of her feet caused by the cold hardwood floors.

A minute later, climbing into bed and drawing the covers up to her neck, she planned on going back to sleep, but unfortunately, the stranger who just happened to be her husband sauntered into the room.

He took the liberty of feeling her forehead, then said, "You don't feel like you have any fever."

"Thank you, doctor."

"You're welcome."

Clutching her stomach, she wished more than anything—even more than she wished Finn would leave her to suffer in private—that she had the heating pad from her apartment, but it was in storage along with the rest of her belongings that she'd planned to have shipped to Dallas's house after their wedding.

"Wait right here," Finn said, heading for the hall. "My aunt knew exactly what to do to make me feel better after I tossed my cookies."

"Let you die in peace?" Lilly muttered.

"I heard that!" he said from the hall.

She heard rustling and guessed the source of the racket to be Finn rummaging through the hall closet.

A few minutes later, he was back, wielding his prize. "Taa-daa."

She'd closed her eyes and now opened them. Could it be? Did Finn really hold in his hands what she thought he did, or was she hallucinating?

"That's a heating pad," she said. "How did you know?"

"How did I know what?" He knelt beside the bedside table to plug it in.

"That whenever I'm sick, that's the one item I can't live without?"

He shrugged. "I know when I was a kid it always made me feel better. I've got an iron stomach now, but…" He pushed back her covers and tenderly set the flannel-covered square against her tummy before pulling the yellow floral comforter back in place. "Well, let's just say this baby got me through some rough times."

"You were sick a lot?"

Finn's jaw hardened as he stared out the window at the fir-dotted foothills surrounding his home. "Not sick in the traditional sense." *Just heartsick over the loss of my parents and sister.*

"Then how?"

He took a deep breath and sighed, turning his gaze back to her. "I'd rather not talk about it, okay?" Skimming her bangs from her forehead, he asked, "Can I get you anything else? Sprite? Saltines? Thick socks?"

Grinning, she said, "You know, Dr. Finn, all of the above sounds surprisingly good."

BY LATER THAT MORNING, Lilly felt strong enough to take a shower and style her hair.

The one thing she couldn't do was dwell on how much of her renewed health was due to Finn's nursing.

Just when she thought she had him pegged as an unredeemable scoundrel, for a split second, she'd almost thought she could care for the man. But then she'd probably feel the same about Donald Duck if he not only brought her a heating pad and pair of his own cozy white socks, but made a trip to the store for pop and crackers.

Forehead furrowed, she slowly descended the stairs and made her way through the entry, down the hall and into the sun-flooded kitchen. Finn stood at the stove, stirring a heavenly smelling concoction in a huge Dutch oven.

"What smells so good?" she asked, stepping behind him for a quick peek.

"I thought my patient could use a bowl of chicken soup for lunch. My aunt swears by this recipe. And I'll have you know I had to call her in Florida to get it."

"You did that for me?"

"Yep, and you owe me for the grief I went through. My aunt couldn't quite grasp the concept of me needing chicken soup to heal my *new* bride."

"I take it she didn't know about your bet?" Lilly pulled out a chair at the kitchen table and had a seat.

"Nope. Her boyfriend had tickets to some fancy

golf tournie in West Palm Beach for Sunday, so she flew back to Miami late Saturday afternoon.''

Looking to her nails, Lilly noted that they needed a fresh coat of polish. Good. Focusing on routine was a great way to keep from asking a zillion more questions about Finn's aunt. "I'm, ah, sorry about what Vivian did to you. That was pretty low.''

He shrugged, set the wooden spoon he'd been using on the blue tile counter. "Surprisingly enough, I'm over it. When it happened, I thought I'd die, but now, I guess her leaving was for the best.''

"How so?'' She looked up and for a second was caught off guard. In all their fussing, she'd forgotten Finn's extraordinary good looks. His square and true jawline. His soul-penetrating dark eyes. And those lips… Her pulse quickened, remembering the feel of them on her breasts.

Swallowing hard, she looked away.

"Easy,'' he said, crossing the room to pull out the chair beside her. "If I'd been married to Vivian right now, I wouldn't be married to you.'' He sat unbearably close. Close enough that if she dared, she could cup his cheek and they'd no longer be strangers, but that perfectly-at-ease couple they'd been in Vegas.

Reminding herself to breathe, Lilly licked her lips. "But you must have loved Vivian terribly if you'd planned to marry her.''

He reached for her hands and why she didn't know, but Lilly let him. "I thought I loved her, but now, I'm not so sure. Maybe I never even knew what love was.''

"And do you now? Know what love is, I mean?''

She boldly met his stare and for a moment time stood still. She felt him searching her face for answers, answers to what she didn't know, and she was terrified of the implications of her asking.

"Maybe."

She swallowed again. "What do you think it would take to make you know for sure?"

"A sign."

"What kind of sign?"

"Something that proves that this time, I'm not putting my faith in the wrong woman."

"Knowing how I feel about the subject of divorce, what will you do if you find I'm not the right woman for you?"

With the pads of his thumbs, Finn caressed the sides of her index fingers. "I think that's the least of our worries, don't you?"

Funny, but from where Lilly was sitting, the heat Finn strummed into her fingers made it feel like just the start of her worries!

Chapter Nine

The next morning, Lilly rose cautiously, testing her equilibrium before committing to action. But even that motion was evidently too much. Her stomach roiled and once again, the mad dash to the bathroom was on.

Blech.

Once again, she made it in time, but didn't manage to shut the door.

"Good Lord, woman," Finn said a few seconds later, kneeling beside her with his hands cupped around her shoulders. "I thought we had this thing licked, but you must have picked up one heck of a bug."

When she felt stable enough, Lilly plopped onto her rear, resting her back against the cool claw-footed tub.

"Let me get you a washcloth," he said, already on his way to the sink. He first made her a cold one, then hot.

"How is it," she said, leaning her head against the tub as well, "that you always seem to know what I need?"

He flushed the commode and lowered the lid before taking a seat. "It isn't as if it takes any great psychic powers to know that a sick woman needs looking after.''

"Yeah, well, psychic powers, or not, I appreciate what you've done. I enjoyed the soup last night and…'' She lowered her gaze. "I'm enjoying your company now.''

"It's my pleasure.'' After they sat in silence for a few minutes, Finn softly stroking her hair away from her forehead, he said, "Feel like getting back in bed?''

She nodded, tried grappling to her feet, but before she could, Finn stood beside her, crouching to place one arm beneath her knees and the other behind her shoulders. In a smooth glide, he scooped her into his arms and carried her to her room.

Lilly's mind was so tired and limbs so weak that it didn't even occur to her to fight. Instead, she rested her cheek against his chest, relishing Finn's quiet strength.

Then, tucked in bed with a pile of downy pillows beneath her head, another pair of her husband's thick socks on her feet and Finn in the kitchen fetching her more Sprite and crackers, it once again occurred to Lilly that for a man she'd so callously accused of caring nothing about her feelings, he sure as heck was doing a bang-up job of proving her wrong.

Funny how the men she thought she'd loved—Elliot and Dallas—had turned out to both be creeps, yet the one man she professed to hate…

Memories of the sweet care Finn had taken with her caused her cheeks to flush.

When he returned, he held a sweating glass of clear soda to her lips and helped her take a sip. Setting the glass on the bedside table, he said, "I'm going to call a doctor. It's weird how this thing keeps coming and going. Last night, I thought you were getting better, but this morning—no offense, you look worse than ever."

"Thanks," she said with a feeble grin.

His quick smile stole what little was left of her breath. Beyond being sick, what was happening to her? She wasn't falling for her husband, was she?

"KNOCK KNOCK," Finn said later that afternoon at her bedroom door. "Lilly? Are you decent? I brought company."

"Company?"

She tucked the tattered copy of *What to Expect When You're Expecting* beneath her pillow and straightened in the bed.

Finn ushered in a bright-eyed woman Lilly guessed to be in her early fifties. Her hair was styled in a chic blond bob and she wore tailored navy slacks and a matching blazer over a white silk blouse. An elegant strand of pearls hung at her throat and in her right hand she clutched a classic black leather doctor's bag.

Lilly's heart pounded. *A doctor's bag?*

Oh no, was her secret blown?

"Hello," the woman said with a kind smile, setting her bag on the foot of the bed, then holding out her right hand. "You must be Lilly. I'm Dr. Walsh."

"Nice to meet you," Lilly said, returning the woman's firm grip and hoping the physician hadn't noticed the sudden sweating of her patient's palm.

"But I told Finn that I'm feeling much better and don't need a doctor."

"That's okay," the woman said, reaching into her bag to pull out a stethoscope. "I live up the road, so it was no big deal for me to stop by on my way home. Now, can you tell me what seems to be the problem?"

Drawing her lower lip into her mouth, Lilly looked from the doctor to her husband, who had made himself at home on the empty half of the bed.

"She hardly keeps anything down, Doc."

"Um, Finn," Lilly summoned the nerve to say. "Do you mind if I have a few moments alone with the doctor? This is after all, kind of a private thing."

"What do you need privacy for to be checked out for the flu? I should be here just in case. Right, Doc Walsh?"

"Wrong. Skedaddle," the doctor said with a wave of her manicured hands. "Lilly's right. We women don't always need our men listening in." When Finn finally left, closing the door firmly behind him, the doctor said, "You had something to tell me in private?"

Swallowing hard, Lilly nodded. "I'm, um, pretty sure I'm not really sick…just pregnant."

The doctor gasped. "How wonderful! Our Finn's finally going to be a daddy!" Lowering her voice, she said, "Sorry for the unprofessional outburst, it's just that for as long as I can remember, Finn has been caring for everything around here from those stray dogs of his to elementary-school kids. Finn Reilly will make the best father imaginable."

While that was certainly great news to Lilly, the fact

still remained that Finn wasn't *her* baby's father. Sure, most any man would love his own child, but to love another man's child? That took a special breed.

Narrowing her eyes, the doctor checked Lilly's blood pressure. "Why do I get the feeling there's something else you aren't telling me?"

"The, ah…" Lilly looked to the door, confirming that it was solidly closed. "The baby isn't Finn's. In fact, he doesn't even know I'm pregnant."

"Oh?"

"Our marriage isn't exactly a match made in heaven. We met in a pretty unorthodox way."

The doctor glanced at her slim gold watch. "I have almost an hour until my husband has supper on the table. I'm sensing you carry a burden you'd like to get off your chest, but please, if that isn't the case, know you won't offend me by telling me to mind my own business." Her genuinely warm smile put Lilly at ease while the doctor settled onto the rocker Finn had placed at the head of her bed.

"No," Lilly said. "You're right. I guess I have been hungering for another woman's point of view." Being careful to only convey facts and not to lay blame, Lilly shared every detail about how she and Finn had come to be married.

"Hmm, that *was* quite a story," the doctor said when Lilly finished. She leaned forward in her chair. "I see how telling Finn about your baby could be rough, but believe me," she said, taking Lilly's right hand in hers and giving it a gentle squeeze, "I've known Finn since he was a boy. He's been through so much pain, and deserves so much happiness. You'll never find a better husband for you, or father for your baby. But as attentive and respectful as he'll be to you and your child, you owe him that same respect. I was at his wedding when Vivian walked out. I saw the anguish in his eyes. Right now, talk around town is that he trusts you implicitly. Were he to lose faith in you as he did Vivian, I'm not sure how he'd react.'' She took a deep breath and sighed. ''Lilly, in my professional and personal opinion, I think you should tell him the truth—preferably before he makes a few deductions of his own.''

IN THE KITCHEN, Finn was pouring a cup of coffee when the doctor said, ''Your bride is going to live.''

His shoulders sagged with relief. ''What's wrong with her? Should I go get her some medicine?''

''No, I don't think she needs a thing other than a nice, long rest.'' Gesturing to Finn's mug, she said, ''Would you mind pouring me a cup? We have to talk.''

''That doesn't sound good,'' he said, snatching another blue mug from the rack hanging beneath the cabinets. ''There *is* something seriously wrong with her, isn't there? I knew this whole almost-wedded-bliss thing was too good to be true. She's dying, isn't she? How long do we have?'' As he poured the coffee into the mug, his hands trembled and he spilled some of the scalding liquid onto his hand. ''Dammit. Why is it that when I find someone I think I could love, they either run off or die on me, Doc?''

''Oh, Finn.'' She crossed the room to envelope him in a laughing hug. ''I'm sorry for planting that seed in your head. Lilly has nothing medically wrong with her. What I want to discuss is the way you met.'' Releasing him, she took a step back to wag her finger in his face. ''I wanted to say, shame on you for ever accepting Mitch's bet in the first place.'' She shook her head. ''You know better.''

A second rush of relief turned Finn's knees to jelly. ''I'll gladly take your scolding and then some, just promise you'll never scare me like that again.''

''I promise.'' She stepped to the counter to add cream and sugar to her coffee. ''Since you've been like one of my own sons for as long as I can remember, Finn, I'll tell you what does scare me about Lilly.''

''What's that?''

They both took seats at the table.

''The suddenness with which this whole marriage came about. She seems like a sweet woman, but you do realize that just because she feels morally bound to the marriage, that doesn't mean you have to agree? You deserve the entire package, Finn. Happily ever after with all the trimmings.'' Placing her hand on his, she added, ''Are you sure Lilly is the woman who will make all those dreams of yours come true?''

Flashing his longtime friend a smile, Finn said, ''That's the strangest part. Yeah, I think she is my dream woman. Before either of us knew who the other was, we had a chemistry I can't begin to describe. And at the moment we said our vows, I had the craziest feeling that I really did want to be with her for the rest of my life.''

"Even though you hadn't yet known her a full day?"

Leaning back in his chair, he sighed. "Doc, as hard as I've tried denying it, I wanted to marry Lilly after being with her for only ten minutes."

The older woman beamed. "That's all I needed to know. In that case," she said, pulling him into a quick hug. "I guess congratulations are in order."

Wincing, Finn said, "I'm afraid your well wishes are premature."

"For heaven's sake, why? You've already admitted to being head over heels for her and I can't imagine why any woman wouldn't feel the same about you."

"That's just it," he said. "She can't stand me."

"Oh, apple dumplings. I don't believe it for a second."

"It's true. She can't get past the fact that I only married her to win a bet."

"Well, then it seems to me your job is clear. You have to make her get over it."

"How? Matt said to woo her with flowers and candy and stuff, but she's been so sick, all I've been able to do is bring her Sprite and crackers—oh, and a heating pad."

The doctor's smile grew even brighter.

"What? I know it's corny, but she really did like it."

"Of course, she did. A woman like Lilly doesn't want flowers—well, I'm sure she'd enjoy the occasional dozen roses—but what I suspect she truly wants is security. The knowledge that she'll always find a home in your arms."

Finn laughed. "Right. How am I supposed to make her feel all that when she won't come near any part of me, let alone my arms?"

Leaning forward with her elbows on the table, the doctor said, "Here's what you're going to do."

FRIDAY MORNING, a quick glance outside—not to mention the nip in the air—told Lilly that their streak of luck with unseasonably warm weather was over. Driving rain pebbled the windowpanes and clouds hung low to the ground, making it seem as if a huge gray lid had been placed on the usually expansive view.

On the table beside her, an antique clock ticked, but Lilly was so afraid of suffering another bout of nausea that she didn't even want to look at the time. She needn't have looked anyway, though. The grandfather clock chimed ten.

Ugh, she thought, pushing a few stray curls clear of her eyes, she'd never been prone to sleeping this late. Married life and motherhood were turning her into a slug.

Since her battle with morning, afternoon and evening sickness, Finn had been extraordinarily kind. Always seeing to it that the few creature comforts that brought her relief were on hand the instant she needed them. Even better than all the Sprite, saltines, and socks he'd supplied, was his being there. Not since she'd been a kid staying home sick from school had she felt so utterly cared for. And she had to admit, seeing this nurturing side of Finn was going a long way toward changing her attitude about him.

Could he truly be the man she'd fallen for in Vegas?

A knock sounded on the door. "Hello?"

Just hearing Finn's voice made her heart flutter.

"Sleeping Beauty? You awake in there?"

"Barely."

"Are you at least decent?"

"Yes."

"Damn," he said, creaking open the door. His rakish grin was all it took to turn her gray skies blue. "I was hoping to see a little skin."

She touched her palms to her cheeks. "You mean this battleship-green stuff that used to be my complexion?"

"You look gorgeous to me."

"Thanks. Flattery will get you everywhere."

When he perched beside her, it dawned on Lilly how comfortable they'd become over the past few days. "So, sicky? Feel like getting out of bed?"

"I'm not sure. So far I feel pretty good, but I'm afraid if I move I'll end up in another race for the commode."

"How about if I carry you to the living room sofa? Think you'd be all right there?"

The mere prospect of being in his arms brought instant pleasure, which she quickly squelched. Lowering her eyes, lest he see the heat that had risen to her cheeks, she said, "Thanks for the offer of transport, but I can probably make it on my own. Why?"

His only answer was a maddening grin. "Pull on some sweats and meet me downstairs. I have a surprise."

Chapter Ten

For the life of him, Finn couldn't figure out what the doc's plan was supposed to accomplish, but he was willing to give it a try. Matt's sister, Rachel, had been pretty keen on the idea, too.

After making the drop-off—a thirty-minute process by the time they'd unloaded all the gear from the mini-van—Finn was already exhausted, but it was a good exhaustion. One he hoped would get even better by day's end.

"Lilly?" He hollered up the stairs. "Are you dressed yet? I could really use your help."

"Coming!" she shouted from the upstairs hall. "Let me put my hair in a ponytail and brush my teeth."

Finn glanced at the jumble of pink stuff cluttering his living room, then shouted, "Hurry!"

"I am hurrying," she finally said at the top of the stairs. "You forget, this is the first time I've walked under my own steam in three whole days. So? Where's the fire?" she asked on the bottom step.

"Surprise…" He pointed toward a lacy pink basket on the river-stone hearth. "We're baby-sitting."

Lilly's mouth dropped open, then she snapped it shut.

Some friend Dr. Walsh had turned out to be. She'd told Finn everything, hadn't she?

Tears started at the back of her throat, spilling from her eyes in two seconds flat. Doing an abrupt about-face, she marched up the stairs as fast as her weakened condition allowed. "How could she do this to me?" she cried. "What ever happened to doctor-patient privilege?"

"What are you talking about?" Finn asked, checking to make sure Abby was still contentedly sleeping, tiny fist in mouth, before chasing Lilly up the stairs. "The doc had nothing to do with this." *Liar.* But why would Lilly suspect Dr. Walsh of playing a part in his plan? "Matt's sister Rachel called this morning and said she had some kind of lady's thing down at her church and that the woman who runs the nursery was at an aunt's funeral in Salt Lake."

"How come Rachel's husband isn't watching her?"

"He's a teacher. He couldn't get off work."

"And you could?"

He shrugged. "I'd already made plans to take this week off for my honeymoon. Remember?" Reaching for her hand, he said, "Come on, help me out, will ya? It'll be fun."

He was encouraged by the fact that she clung to his hand. "Do you promise the doctor didn't put you up to this?"

He gulped. "Sure."

"Okay. I suppose spending the day with a baby would be fun."

"WAAAAAA!"

"What do we do now?" Lilly asked Finn, hoping she didn't look half as panicked as she felt. Why, oh why, didn't babies come with instructions? Cradling squalling Abby to her chest, Lilly patted her tiny back.

"That's it," Finn said. "Burp her. She probably has gas." He warily eyed the half-full jars of baby peas, chicken and blueberries that were supposed to have fed the infant, but somehow more of it had landed on their clothes than in Abby's tummy. "I know if I had to eat that stuff, I'd be feeling under the weather."

"Waaa-waaa-waaa!"

"Finn, do something. Whatever's wrong with her is getting worse. Maybe we should take her to the emergency room?"

Maddeningly calm, he flashed her a grin. "Give me that kid. All she needs is Uncle Finn."

"Waa-huh-waaa!"

"What she needs is a qualified emergency room staff. What if she has internal bleeding? A tumor or blockage?"

Pfft.

"Eeew," Lilly said, wrinkling her nose. "What's that smell?"

Patting Abby's suddenly thicker rump, he said, "I imagine that smell is her *blockage.*" Holding the now-smiling infant at arm's length, he said, "Were you having a Maalox moment, Princess Abby?" Zooming her through the air, he headed for the living room to change her diaper.

"Put her down, Finn." Lilly charged after them. "If

her tummy was already upset, who knows what cruising through the air at subsonic speed could do.''

"Would you relax?" Finn grinned up at her from the changing pad where he'd already removed Abby's diaper and was competently wiping her clean. "I've got this under control. Abby and I are pals. Aren't we, sweetie?" He blew a raspberry on her plump belly.

Collapsing onto the overstuffed washed-denim couch, Lilly watched in awe as her big husband took amazing care of the itty-bitty baby. Realizing that had she been in charge, she'd have already been halfway to the emergency room, her throat tightened. Swiping a few relieved tears from the corners of her eyes, she wondered if now was the time to tell him he was going to have a little bundle all his own?

Well, sort of his own.

She licked her lips. "Um, Finn?"

"Abby, girl," he said, eyeing the baby's muck-encrusted pink jumper. "Instead of putting all this dirty stuff back on you, how about we find out if your pretty face is hiding somewhere under all those peas and blueberries?"

The infant did a coo and gurgle combo that wrenched Lilly's heart.

Tell him, her conscience fairly screamed. *You'll never have a more perfect chance.*

"I'm sorry," Finn said, glancing her way. "Did you say something?"

Summoning a bright smile, she said, "Nope. Want me to gather all her bath gear?"

"Sure. If you feel up to it."

For once, Lilly's body felt fine. Her heart was another matter entirely.

"SHE'S BEAUTIFUL, isn't she?" Lilly snapped Abby's lavender overalls before scooping her up from the bathroom counter to cradle the baby against her shoulder.

"She's a doll all right," Finn said, his heart full at the sight of his beautiful wife and child. Sure, Abby wasn't their baby, but if he had any say in the matter— soon, *very* soon—he and Lilly would start making rugrats of their own. "She's not the only girl in this room I've got my eye on."

Lilly's blue gaze snapped to his.

"I'm talking about you, you know."

"Thanks, but with my hair and clothes coated in pureed peas, I'm sure I've never looked worse."

"You're wrong. See for yourself." His fingers beneath her chin, he steered her gaze toward her reflection in the mirror. No—correction, he wanted her to see all three of them in the mirror. He selfishly wanted her to see that playing house with the right man could be fun. "You look like an angel," he said, not gazing directly at Lilly, but at her mirror image as he wrapped one of the curls that had slipped free of her ponytail round his right pinkie. When he released it, it sprang softly against her cheek. "You make a great toy, you know."

"We should, ah, go downstairs," she said, hastily looking away from both the mirror and him.

"Why?"

"Rachel will be by soon to pick up Abby and we

have a lot of packing to do. There's the swing to dis-
assemble and all the dishes and bottles to wash. If
Rachel shows up with the house looking the way it
does, she'll think we made awful temporary parents."

"And that matters to you? What kind of mom my
friend Rachel thinks you'll one day make?"

"Of course, it matters. Doesn't it matter to you?"

Tucking his hands into his pockets on his way out
the door, he said, "Personally, I could give a flip what
Rachel thinks about my fathering skills. It's you I've
been trying to impress."

Abby's downy-soft hair tucked beneath her chin, the
smell of the freshly soaped and lotioned baby over-
whelming her senses, Lilly didn't know whether Finn
had truly said the words or she'd dreamed them.

As he whistled his way downstairs, she held tight
to the baby and chased after him.

Halfway down the stairs, she shouted, "Finn Reilly,
you can't say a thing like that and then just walk
away!"

"Why not?" he asked, already in the living room.

She followed him in there, too. "Because it leaves
all kinds of questions racing through my mind."

"Like what?" With him on one side of the sofa and
her on the other, he said, "Fire away. I'd be happy to
answer anything you'd like."

She licked her lips and hugged Abby even closer
for support. "Okay, um, why do you care if I think
you'd make a good father?"

Resting his knees on the sofa cushions, he held on
to the back of the sofa for balance. Facing her, his
mouth close enough to her breasts that they swelled

from the heat of his breath, he said, "I care because, even in the short time we've been acquainted, I've grown to care about you, Lilly Reilly. For better or worse, you're my wife. It's important you not only think of me as a good future father, but as a provider, and ultimately, as a man you could grow to love."

"Oh." She drew the lower of her quivering lips into her mouth and nibbled.

"Do you think you ever could?"

"What?"

"Love me?"

"Well, I—"

The doorbell rang, then a muffled voice from outside the front door called out, "Yo, Finn! Open up! It's me!"

"Damn," Finn said, already off the sofa and headed to the door.

"Who is it?" Lilly asked, peering across the living room toward the door.

"Matt."

"That's nice. What with trying to put you to bed, last time he was here we didn't get a chance to talk."

Finn shot her a look before opening the door.

"Hey, man," Matt said, strolling past him to barge right on into the house. "Did you ever ask Lilly if Friday night poker was still—oh, hey, Lilly. How's it going? And I see my little Abster's here, too."

Abby cooed when her uncle tickled her under her chin.

"No," Finn growled. "I didn't ask my wife about poker. And even if I had, you're four hours early."

"Touchy, touchy," Matt said, taking off his coat

and tossing it to the Shaker bench by the door. "I didn't have anything better to do, so I thought I'd help you set up."

LILLY YAWNED, closing the front door on the last of Finn's poker guests. "That was fun," she said, heading for the kitchen to clear the table of cups and sandwich plates.

"You're being sarcastic, right?" Finn cleared one side of the table while she tackled the other.

"Not at all. I have four older brothers, and Saturday nights they played poker in the basement. If one of them had a date, I got to sit in."

"Which explains why you beat the pants off all of us."

"You wouldn't be a sore loser, would you, Finn?"

"Hell, yes," he said, rounding the table. "Fifteen dollars and thirty-seven cents in loose change is hard to come by. How am I going to pay the electric bill?"

"I've got money set aside," she said with a wink. "Just this once I can float you the cash, but it's gonna cost you."

"How much?" he said, stepping even closer.

Was he going to kiss her?

When he didn't, she swallowed hard, ignoring her racing pulse and the voice in the back of her head urging her to demand a shocking fee. "I, um, haven't thought that far," she said, lying through her teeth.

"Yes, you have. You know exactly what you want from me. Spill it."

She snatched a beer mug from the table and tried making a getaway, but her husband was too fast, lassoing her around the waist. Aside from carrying her to bed, or holding a cloth to her forehead when she'd been sick, this was the first time since their night in Vegas that he'd purposely touched her.

In a heartbeat, the night came back. The achingly familiar scent of his breath. The feel of his big, open palms covering her breasts. It was too much. The memories were coming too fast, too intense. If she thought of that night for even a second longer, she'd be in danger of telling him not only what she wanted in payment but ever so much more.

This perfect day had made her drunk on life.

The time with Abby, the hours spent laughing with Finn's friends. It only seemed right they should end the perfect day with the perfect kiss.

"Lilly," her husband said, cinching her close. "If you don't name your price, how can I possibly pay it?"

She licked her lips. Swallowed hard. Was it possible for a woman's heart to beat right out of her chest? Giggling at the mental image, she said, "All right, all right, you've worn me down. A kiss is what I want from you." Hopelessly embarrassed, she closed her eyes. "I know, it's a stupid thing to ask for, isn't it? Especially when we—"

"Hardly know each other?" Finn finished her sentence with his mouth less than the width of a poker card from hers.

Her limbs drugged with an unidentifiable need, she somehow found the energy to nod.

"I think a kiss is a perfectly acceptable demand in light of the pleasure you've given me."

"I have?" she squeaked.

Now he was nodding.

"So, um, what kind of kiss should it be? A polite peck between friends?"

"Does that mean you've started to think of me as a friend?" He touched his mouth to hers so softly, so fleetingly, if it hadn't been for the stirring deep in her soul, she wouldn't have believed he'd touched her at all.

At this moment, her heart cried, remembering not only the way they had been in Vegas, but the way he'd treated her here in his home—their home—*I'm not only thinking of you as a friend, but so much more.* "Y-yes," she said, scarcely trusting herself to speak. "I think of you as my friend."

"Good." He touched his lips to hers again, this time, grazing her with a whispery touch that felt like a warm feather against her lips. "Friendship is good. But do you think we could ever be more than friends?"

He pressed his mouth, that finely tuned instrument of exquisite torture, against her neck, giving her no choice but to arch her head, granting him access to whatever he desired.

Friends. Husband and wife. Lovers…

With each passing day, he was opening her mind and heart to the delicious possibilities their future held in store.

"Lilly?"

"Hmm?"

"You didn't answer my question." His lips hot,

tongue moist, he pressed an urgent, openmouthed kiss to the base of her throat.

"Uh-huh…"

"You do think of me as more than just a friend?"

Oh, yes.

He'd murmured the words into her left ear and the heat of them sent chills scurrying up her spine.

"That's great, sweetie." He pressed one more kiss, an unbearably chaste kiss, to her cheek, then released her. "I'm glad you're starting to feel more comfortable around me." Whistling a happy tune, he strolled out of the kitchen. "Would you mind locking up?" he called over his shoulder. "I'm hitting the sack."

GRRR.

Lilly gave her pillow a good punch before wedging it beneath her head.

That mind reader she called a husband had known all along she wanted a kiss. The big creep.

Why did he have to be so handsome? And nice? And sexy? And even good at changing diapers?

Was there nothing the man couldn't do?

Staring out the window at the starless night, for the first time since stepping foot in Finn's house, she realized it was starting to feel like home. She liked the layout of the kitchen and the way all the tea towels and dishcloths matched. It was almost as if Finn had readied this house for a wife years before they ever met.

A pang shot through her heart.

Of course, he'd readied this house for a wife. Vivian. Who knew, maybe she'd been the one to add all the decorative touches that made the house such a welcoming home?

Ugh, this line of thought was crazy.

Vivian's loss was Lilly's gain. Finn Reilly was a wonderful man. By the hour—no, minute—he attracted her more than Elliot or Dallas combined. And seeing Finn interact with Abby proved that what Dr. Walsh had said about him one day being a great father was true.

What else had the doctor said might be true?

Were he to lose faith in you as he did Vivian, I'm not sure how he'd react.

Squeezing her eyes shut tight, Lilly fought a wave of panic. She had to tell Finn about her baby. A half-dozen moments this afternoon, the timing couldn't have been more perfect. So why hadn't she summoned the nerve?

Fear.

Plain and simple, she was terrified of losing him. If he didn't want to raise Elliot's baby, she'd understand. He had every right to desire children of his own.

If Finn left her, not only would she be raising a baby all alone, but she'd have to bear the shame of her disapproving family. And it was that fear which had prompted her to seek a husband in the first place.

Perhaps even worse than all those other fears combined was that the past few days with Finn had felt so gloriously right. Her marriage to Dallas would have been based upon mutual convenience, but she suspected that if she gave Finn half a chance, their marriage could be based upon love.

What would become of her if she were to toss wide-open the doors of her heart to this man? What if telling him about her baby, far from pleasing him, gave him cause to send her packing? Could she bear the pain?

No.

Which was why, even though she knew telling Finn was the right thing, the *only* thing, for her to do in order to base their burgeoning relationship upon mutual trust, she couldn't.

Not yet.

But soon.

Cupping her hands to her womb, she felt not the stirring of her child but the ticking of a clock. Just as her affection for Finn was growing, so was this baby. And with every passing day, her window of opportunity to come clean with her husband passed as well.

"WHAT ARE YOU DOING?" Lilly asked Finn the next morning in the kitchen.

"What's it look like I'm doing?" he said, patting the side of an old-fashioned wicker basket. The inside was lined with red gingham and even had matching red plastic cups secured to the side with worn leather straps. "I'm packing a picnic lunch."

The previous day's storm had passed and Indian summer was back, flooding the room with golden sun that washed away Lilly's nighttime fears and filled her heart with hope.

"Can I help?"

"Sure. Grab a couple apples and some pop from the fridge." He'd just finished piling shaved deli ham on two pieces of wheat bread.

"Where are we going?" she asked from inside the fridge.

"It's a surprise."

"Oh no," she said. "As much fun as I had yesterday, this doesn't involve Abby again, does it?"

Slapping cheese and the top piece of bread on the sandwiches, he said, "Thankfully, no. That little angel wore me out."

"So then?" she said, setting the drinks and fruit in the basket. "Why the mystery?"

He shocked her with a sweet kiss to the tip of her nose. "I like a little mystery now and then. Adds spice to life."

"All right, I'll willingly go along on this magical mystery tour of yours under one condition."

"What's that?"

"Do you also promise we won't be seeing any poodle or parrot juggling?"

"Promise," he said, crossing his heart before setting the sandwiches into the basket beside bags of chips and cookies. Looking at their meal, he frowned. "There's something I forgot, but I can't remember what."

"Hmm," Lilly teased. "Could it be the kitchen sink?"

"Har-de-har-har. Oh, I know. The wine."

Wine?

She couldn't drink. Alcohol was bad for the baby, but how was she going to explain that to Finn?

Again Dr. Walsh's words haunted her. …*you should tell him the truth—preferably before he makes a few deductions of his own.*

Chapter Eleven

"That's, okay," Lilly said, "I've never been all that big on wine. Gives me a headache."

"Really? This is good stuff. Made locally. You sure you don't want to at least give it a try?"

She shook her head.

"All right, then. Let me grab a couple of sweatshirts and we'll head out."

The ride to their mystery destination couldn't have been more relaxing. Finn was the consummate host, pointing out spots of interest along the way and sharing funny stories about his childhood. The one thing he never brought up were his parents, and though Lilly wondered why, she figured her husband had his reasons and left it at that.

Greenleaf was nestled in the foothills of the Wasatch Mountains and with each foot in elevation Abigail climbed, the sweeter became the air and view. Majestic firs lined the winding road and snow-covered peaks cradled glistening sapphire jewels far too pretty to be called mere lakes.

Finally Finn pulled the truck off the paved highway and onto a dirt road that was more of a track.

"Now I'm getting suspicious," she said. "This doesn't look like any picnic ground I've ever seen."

"Just wait." Holding tight to the wheel, he steered the truck around tooth-jarring potholes. "I promise, the destination is well worth this rough ride."

"I hope so," she said, shooting him a grin. "Dentures don't come cheap!"

True to his word, ten minutes later, her husband parked Abigail in an alpine meadow. Tall grasses swayed in a light breeze and when Lilly climbed out of the truck, she was first struck by the difference in temperature, and then by the quiet and smells. The air was crisp, and clean enough to have a taste. Spicy firs, sweet late-blooming alpine willow weed, and the thirst-quenching scent of water from a pond about a hundred yards to the north, its rippled surface reflecting the grandeur of a neighboring, snowcapped peak.

"That's Mount Neebo," Finn said, climbing out of the truck to stand beside her.

"Why's it called that?"

He shrugged. "As kids, we used to call it Mount *Neemo* after the famous submarine captain."

"Makes sense."

"You ready for a hike?"

"That depends. We're not climbing Mount Neebo-Neemo, are we?"

"What's the matter, Mrs. Reilly? You're not chicken, are you?"

Not only that, but every minute I happen to be falling a little more for you, Mr. Reilly. If they had their picnic in the meadow, not only could they be lazy, but she'd have more time to stare at him. In teasing her, he'd lightly wrapped his arm about her shoulders and flashed her his widest smile of strong, white teeth. His eyes shone the deepest shade of brown, reminding her of other yummy brown things such as cocoa and Hershey bars. As if all that weren't enough, there was his body to contend with. His broad shoulders and washboard abs, clad in a faded green Greenleaf High T-shirt, and his long, strong legs in worn 501s. Whew, she'd married quite a stud.

"Bawk, bawk," she finally said once she'd recovered from the gorgeous view—the view of her husband, that is! "Can't we eat here in the meadow? That long ride was tiring, and I am kind of hungry."

"No way are you getting off that easy. I brought you up here for a reason." At the back of the truck, he pulled their basket from the bed. "Come on, woman, march."

"Where to? That lovely boulder over there?" Sweetly smiling, she pointed to a rock not three feet from the truck's chrome fender.

"Nice try. Thatta way." He pointed to a well-used trail winding into a stand of firs and golden-leafed aspen.

The hike was taxing, yet the beauty more than made up for Lilly's aching joints. In the years since she'd been to the mountains, she'd forgotten how much fun a day spent communing with nature could be. The pungent scent of evergreens invigorated her senses. The sight of sunbeams slanting through feathery pine boughs invigorated her soul.

"This is my favorite part of the hike," Finn said,

slowing to match her pace while enfolding her hand in his. "It feels like a church, don't you think?"

"Mmm-hmm." She gave his hand a knowing squeeze.

They hiked about ten more minutes, cushy pine needles absorbing their footsteps and voices, then emerged from the forest and into another meadow. At the far end, massive pine timbers framed the opening to a mine shaft that had been blasted into the face of a rocky bluff.

Stopped at the head of the trail, Lilly put her hands on her hips. "Why does this scene strike me as familiar?"

His grin looked the teeniest bit guilty. "Beats me."

"Finn Reilly, fess up. Is this the same mine where you took Shannon Jowoskiwitz in the hopes of scoring?"

Aiming his gaze toward the blazing blue sky, he said, "Could be. If it is, I'm too much of a gentleman to ever tell." With a brazen wink, he added, "I'm impressed. You remembered her name."

"That's not all I remember. I know firsthand what you like doing in caves." The moment she said the words, Lilly put her hand to her mouth. That last thought was supposed to have only been for her!

Her husband set their basket at his feet before crossing the short distance to where she stood. Hands loosely on her hips, he said, "Seems to me I wasn't the only one who enjoyed our game of cave explorer."

Trying to hide her smile, she pushed free of his hold. "Yeah, well, that was when I thought I knew you."

"Are we back to that old excuse?"

"What's that supposed to mean?" She spun to face him. "It's the truth, Finn. That night, I thought you were Dallas. If I hadn't, I never would have…well, let's just say we would have had separate rooms and leave it at that."

"I'd rather leave it at this…."

Hands back on her hips, he tugged her close. Too close. Her traitorous body instinctively melded against him. Her coursing pulse muddled her normally good judgment. Before she could tell him to slow down, he pressed his lips to hers for the sweetest of kisses. No pressure, just promises. Promises that he'd give her the life she'd always wanted. Babies and a wonderful home and good friends and the respect of her always perfect siblings and parents.

All too soon, he released her and, without his support, she felt fragile as dandelion fluff being ferried by the wind. It was at that moment, when she realized without his arms around her she no longer knew which direction her life should go, that she made the heart-stopping realization that she could be falling in love with him. The bet no longer mattered. Truth be told, he'd been as confused about their meeting as she had. All that mattered now was that they were meant for each other in every conceivable way from them both liking hamburgers for breakfast to the fact that she was a perfect fit in his arms.

All she had to do was tell him about her baby and their lives would be complete. If he felt half for her what she did for him, he'd welcome her child with loving arms. He could have insisted upon obtaining a divorce, but he hadn't. He'd stuck by her and she could only pray he'd stick by her baby as well.

"Are you ready to enter Finn's Cave of Love?" he teased, holding her with one hand and the basket with the other.

"Is it safe?" she said, her maternal instincts overriding those dying to once again be in the dark, alone with her husband.

"Absolutely. I bring scout troops up here every year, so each fall I have a structural engineering buddy help me shore it up."

"You do a lot for kids, don't you?"

"What can I say? I'm a sucker for the little buggers."

Tell him now, her heart urged. *You'll never have a better chance to break the news about your baby.*

He led her into the mine shaft and it took a second for her eyes to adjust to the change in light. The temperature dropped ten degrees and the musty smell transported her to a time when the place would have bustled with men seeking their fortunes.

Again Finn set down the basket. This time though, he opened the lid and withdrew a navy-blue sweatshirt and powerful flashlight.

Holding the shirt up to her, he said, "Lift your arms and I'll put this on for you."

She did as he asked, luxuriating in the feel of his expert care. His knuckles grazed the sides of her breasts, tickling her with an erotic jolt. "Thanks for thinking of me," she said.

"Hey," he flashed her his sexiest grin. "I learned

the hard way, through Shannon, that cold girls are a lot less likely to put out.''

She made a face. ''Is you-know-what all you ever think about, Finn Reilly?''

Drawing her close for a swift kiss, he said, ''It is when I'm with you, Lilly Reilly. So how about it? Care to get lucky in an old silver mine?''

Her heart flip-flopping with what she half hoped and half feared was love for this incredibly tender, sweet and sexy man, Lilly said, ''Lead the way. You never know what treasure we might find.''

''THIS PLACE IS like something out of another world…''

After following a maze of tunnels, they'd entered a cavernous room complete with stalactite chandeliers and an orchestra of dripping water. Crystals sparkled in the flashlight's powerful beam, and the surface of most rocks had taken on a pale, milky glow. Stone pillars formed a natural gate to a clear lake and where most caves she'd been in had smelled as if a bear had been using it as his winter condo, this one smelled fresh, of water and soil, and miners' faded dreams.

''From what I've read about these kinds of rock formations,'' Finn said, ''we practically are in another world. For Utah, this is pretty amazing stuff.'' Finn found himself once again swelling with manly pride. He loved making Lilly happy, and to think that she was enjoying this unique spot as much as he did made the moment that much more special.

''Shannon Jowoskiwitz was crazy not to have kissed you in here.''

"That's what I thought," he said, kneeling to light an oil lamp he kept stashed in the room. "But since her rejection, you're the first girl I've brought back."

Pressing her hands to his chest, she said, "In spite of my cold nose, I'm honored. So?" she asked, lightly stepping from one side to the other of the gurgling stream feeding the lake, "When do I get my kiss?"

"Patience, my dear. No kissing until after we dine." On a massive flat stone, he arranged their picnic atop a red flannel blanket.

After the long hike, Lilly was plenty hungry and never had sandwiches tasted so good. "You're a great cook," she said.

"Thanks. I've been using this top-secret recipe for years. Honey ham and provolone. Don't tell a soul." Even in the wavering lamplight, she saw his eyes sparkle with devilish charm.

"Why didn't you ever bring Vivian here?" she asked after taking a drink of frosty root beer.

He shrugged. "She was pretty high maintenance. Spending an afternoon traipsing around an old mine wasn't her cup of tea. Come to think of it," he said, popping his last bite of sandwich into his mouth. "We never had that much in common."

"Then why did you ask her to marry you?"

Finn frowned. Was now the time to tell his wife how desperate he'd been to start a family? How weary he'd been of casual dating? "She was gorgeous and said she loved me. I guess I naively thought the rest would work itself out." Snatching a Nutter Butter, he asked, "Speaking of our exes, you never did tell me how Dallas took the news that you'd gotten hitched."

"At first he was nice, said he'd been worried about me. But then I told him what had happened between you and me and he turned cold. Said some pretty harsh things."

"Sorry." Giving her hand a squeeze, Finn said, "I know back in Vegas you thought the guy hung the moon. Discovering you'd rather kick him *to* the moon must've hurt."

"Yeah, well…" Her lips curved in a slight grin, she shrugged. "Honestly, I think it's best he showed his true colors. When I first found out that you weren't him, I toyed with the idea of divorcing you to go ahead and marry him."

"So? What stopped you?" Waiting for her answer, Finn's heart caught in his throat.

"Principle. I remembered I already was married. As you'll find out when you meet my folks over Thanksgiving, they're all about family. Perfect family. There's never been a divorce in our family tree and I wasn't about to be the first to break a branch."

"Even though following that so-called perfect example may mean spending your entire life in a loveless marriage?"

She swallowed hard. "Who said ours was destined to be a loveless marriage?"

"Don't tease me about something like that, Lilly."

"I'm not. These past few days have, well…you've showed me in a hundred tiny ways what kind of man you truly are. I love how you buy ice cream for Chrissy and Randy. I love how you cared for me when I was sick and for Rachel's baby when she needed a sitter. You're constantly caring for everyone around you, Finn Reilly, but never yourself."

Not knowing what to say, he remained silent.

"Well, you know what?" she asked, silently clearing a path in their remaining food to creep to his side of the blanket.

"What?"

"It's about time someone started caring for you, and I nominate…me." In the dancing lamplight, she kissed him. Soft at first, testing, seeing if he understood what she'd been trying to say. But then he groaned and slid his work-roughened hand under the fall of her hair. Leaning back, he pulled her on top of him. And then there was no more need for words when their actions spoke eloquently for them both.

Finn sighed, drawing strength from the woman he found more intriguing by the moment. What an amazing twist of fate meeting her had been. "I know this may sound crazy, but knowing that you're now one hundred percent committed to our marriage is such a turn-on. So is knowing you'd never even think of hurting me like Vivian."

"Oh, Finn…" *Tell him about the baby,* Lilly's conscience urged. *Before it's too late.*

He took her half-crazed moan to mean that she was ready for more kissing, and when he proceeded to do just that, she felt powerless to stop.

Being with him felt so good, so right.

It wouldn't have mattered if they were in this cave or on Mars, she never wanted to be anyplace other than in his arms. But therein lay the problem. What if she told him the truth about her baby and he rejected her? What if she not only had to deal with her family's disapproval, but the heartache of losing her husband?

His voice hoarse from emotion, he said, "I want to make love with you. Right here, right now."

Resting her cheek against his chest, she heard the thunder of his heart. "I want that, too," she said. "You'll never know how much, but I can't."

"Why?"

"I—"

"Look at me, Lilly." He leaned back, granting himself a view deep into her eyes. She might have been fully clothed, but his stare made her feel stripped to her soul. "I just admitted how much I care for you. I thought you felt the same?"

"I do, it's just that—"

"What? Why don't you want to..."

Lilly fought for air. Though his words trailed off, they both knew what he meant.

Time. She needed time to figure out how to best tell him about the baby. Then they'd make love, because only then would her affection be coming from a pure place.

"Lilly?"

She sighed. "Please, Finn, don't spoil what has been a beautiful day. I promise you, we will make love again, but I need more space. Admitting the extent to which I've grown to care for you was a big step. Making love to you will be even bigger. We've already come so far. Please, *please* be patient just a short while longer."

THAT EVENING, Finn turned off the downstairs lights and was climbing the stairs when Lilly realized she had a tough decision to make.

The night had turned blustery. Outside, a fierce wind sent branches scurrying against the windows, begging to be let in. The wind's lonely howl reminded her how more than anything, she wanted to join her husband in his big bed, spending dark hours cuddled in the light of his arms, but her heart wouldn't let her.

She hadn't yet told him about the baby and with every passing minute, she grew more terrified of what his reaction might be. If she resumed her marital relations with him and he did send her packing once he heard her news, wouldn't the fact that they'd been a husband and wife in every sense of the word make her leaving that much harder?

Pausing at the top of the stairs, Finn said, "Come to bed with me, Lilly."

"Finn, I—"

"We don't have to do anything you don't want. We'll talk. Hold each other."

Her lower lip started to quiver and she longed for the strength to hold her tears at bay. "I wish I could share a bed with you, but I can't."

"Why?"

"I'm not ready. I told you, I need more time."

"Time for what? What is time going to do other than make what we're feeling that much stronger?"

"Nothing, I—"

"What, Lilly?" His fingers beneath her chin, he held her gaze steady on his. "What aren't you telling me? Are you still upset over the part I played in that stupid bet?"

No. "Yes, okay? You say you feel you can trust me, but I still need to trust you." *Trust you not to break my heart when I shock you with my news.*

"But I thought. This afternoon, the things you said..."

"I meant every word, but can't you see? I need more time to process all of this, what I'm feeling. It came about so quickly. My mind is spinning. Please," she said, pressing her hands to his chest. "Please, Finn, give me room to think."

"Okay." He pressed a tender kiss to her lips. "But as of now, consider yourself on notice."

"For what?" she asked, her heart thudding with dread when he took her hands in his.

"Notice that I'm about to make you the happiest, most contented woman who ever lived. Mark my words, by Thanksgiving, you are going to not only be sharing my bed, but every aspect of my life."

Promise?

He pulled her close for a mind-shattering kiss that not only weakened her knees but her resolve. Yes, she should go with him, to his bed, to his soul...anywhere he wanted to go.

"Before I forget," he said, releasing her to fish in the front pocket of his jeans. "I meant to give this to you today, but the timing wasn't right." He pressed a plastic key chain and key into her open palm, then closed her fingers around it.

"What does this unlock?" she asked.

"Nothing much. Just my home and heart. Good night," he said, his breath hot against her swollen lips.

"Good night."

In the shadowy hall, she felt rather than saw his gaze, and then he slipped away, entering his room and quietly shutting the door.

Take me with you, her heart cried as she squeezed the cold key until it sliced into her skin, but her conscience reigned supreme.

Opening her fingers, in the dim light of the hall sconce, she studied the plastic key chain. It was a big red Sparky the Wonder Dog souvenir, and on the back, Finn had engraved *How about adding me and Sparky to your key chain collection?*

She'd forgotten all about the surprise he'd purchased for her in Vegas. Despite its minimal cost, never had a gift touched her more.

Instantly her old friends the tears were back and she sniffed her way to her room, shut the door and climbed into bed. The sheets were cold and a pine bough swept incessantly against her window.

Tell him, the howling wind urged, never giving her a moment's peace. *Tell him the truth. He's a compassionate man. He'll understand.*

But for every argument in favor of telling him, there was a stronger one against.

What if she told him and he rejected her completely? Thought her despicable for having an affair?

Yes, but you didn't know Elliot was married until it was too late. Elliot told you he loved you and you believed with all your heart you loved him.

Okay, but what if Finn wants nothing to do with raising another man's child?

Nonsense. Finn loves every child. He would never

reject an innocent baby any more than he would reject you.

On and on her turmoil raged, as did the ceaseless wind.

She would tell him in the morning.

She wouldn't tell him in the morning.

Like plucking petals from a daisy, the decision went around and around her head. Sometime after the grandfather clock chimed twelve, still clenching Finn's key in her hand, sheer exhaustion granted Lilly sleep, but even in her dreams she was unable to find peace.

If anything, her dreams of what might have been, made the agony of what would most likely happen hurt all the more. Once she told her husband the truth about why she'd been so eager to not only get married, but stay married, he might never speak to her again.

Chapter Twelve

The two weeks leading to Thanksgiving were the happiest of Finn's life. Yes, the times he'd spent with his parents and sister would always hold a bittersweet place in his heart, but this time with Lilly was different. Not just about cherishing old memories, but making new ones.

The weather had finally changed for good and with each passing day, Old Man Winter knocked harder on their door.

Every afternoon after work, Finn returned home to find Lilly singing show tunes at the stove. She was an amazing cook, and after the two of them lingered at the table discussing their day, he'd build a fire in the living room hearth to warm them as they whiled away the hours until bedtime playing Scrabble or cards, or sometimes doing nothing at all besides lounging in each other's arms, staring into the flames.

The only thing still troubling Finn about their marriage was that Lilly refused to move into his bedroom. He could care less about the sexual aspects of her move. It was the lack of trust that bothered him, the lack of intimacy holding each other through the night would bring.

The day he'd taken her to the mine, he'd been certain they'd reached a changing point in their relationship, and they had, but now he had to wonder how much further they had to go?

Finn wanted all of Lilly, but evidently, that was more than she was ready to give. Still, that was okay. He'd waited a lifetime to find her and if that was what it took to keep her, he'd wait a lifetime more. She meant everything to him. He'd give her all the time she needed to insure she never felt pressured.

"You're going to adore my family," she said to him over a delicious spaghetti dinner the night before Thanksgiving. Outside, cold rain nipped at the windows, but inside, the tropical blue heat of Lilly's eyes made Finn all warm and toasty. "I can't wait for you to meet my brothers and sisters."

"You think I'll fit in?" he asked, his mind spinning at the prospect that he was about to go from having almost no family to so much family he'd have a tough time learning all their names.

"How could they not like you?" she said, setting down her glass of milk to give his hand a reassuring squeeze. "You treat me like royalty and that's all that matters to them."

"Does that mean," he said after swallowing a bite of spaghetti, "you're starting to feel comfortable here, princess? Like this is your castle?"

Not trusting herself to speak, Lilly nodded. If only Finn knew how comfortable she truly felt, and how terrified she was of her deep contentment being snatched away.

After dinner, since she'd cooked, Finn had established firm rules about him cleaning up.

While she sipped an after-dinner cup of peppermint tea, he not only washed dishes but entertained her with hilarious stories about his construction jobs.

Finished washing the last dish, he held out his hand and said, "Mrs. Reilly, shall we retire to the living room?"

"By all means," she said, taking his hand and letting him guide her out of the room.

In the cozy cinnamon-red living room, while Finn built a fire in the river-stone hearth, Lilly took her usual spot at the end of the washed-denim sofa. The cushions were sinkers—meaning they were so comfy that once she plopped down, she was loath to get back up. Which explained how more than a few times she'd fallen asleep, only to wake being carried to bed in her husband's arms.

Adding to the room's warmth were built-in bookshelves lined with current bestsellers and classics. After the first frost, Finn had brought in the porch ferns and they now sat in elegant brass stands tucked into the living room's corners, and throughout the house.

"What's your pleasure?" Finn asked when the fire merrily crackled, fighting off the outside chill. "TV? Letting me beat you at a game of Scrabble?"

"You've never beaten me at a game of Scrabble."

He winked. "That's because I've been letting you win."

"Oh, sure. And that same losing instinct is why it

was so important to you to win that bet against Mitch?''

''Ha-ha. Okay, you got me. I'm a loser when it comes to word games, but do you dare play me a game of Monopoly?''

''That depends,'' she said, stretching like a lazy cat. ''Do you deliver?''

He rolled his eyes. ''Woman, if I let you, you'd be in bed by seven every night of the week.''

''And your point is?'' she said with a wide grin.

''You're hopeless.'' While returning her smile, he shook his head before digging the Monopoly game from the bottom tier of the bookshelf.

Within the hour, Finn was beating her soundly. ''Is this some kind of Scrabble revenge thing you have going?'' she asked, for the third time landing on Baltic Avenue, and having to pay rent on his supposedly low-budget motel.

''Just pay me your four hundred and fifty bucks and quit whining,'' he said, fanning himself with a stack of orange five-hundred-dollar bills.

She mortgaged all her property, counted her meager amount of cash, yet it still wasn't enough. ''I can't pay. You wiped me out.''

''Already?''

''*Already?* You've been trouncing me for the past thirty minutes and you're complaining that it hasn't been long enough?''

A playful sparkle in his deep brown eyes, he leaned across the coffee table, toppling his red-and-green empire to press a kiss to her lips. ''Ouch,'' he said, rubbing his back as he lowered himself to the floor. "I'm getting too old for stealing quick kisses."

"Want me to give you a massage?"

His eyebrows lifted. "Would you? My back hurts *really* bad."

Already rising from the sofa, she said, "Why do I get the distinct impression I'm being bamboozled?"

"'Cause you are?" Finn's rakish grin didn't look the slightest bit sorry as he rolled onto his stomach on the thick rag rug in front of the fire.

"Great," she said, kneeling beside him.

"Hey, can you blame a guy for wanting a rubdown after a long day's work?"

"No, I can't, which is why I'm down here, rubbing you all over, you big lug."

"Mmm…" Her small hands worked magic on his lower and middle back. "Rub me all over, wife. I do like the sound of that."

"You would." She gave him an extra hard squeeze.

"Hey, what'd you do that for? I took good care of you when you were sick."

"Yeah, but I really was sick."

"I am, too. My back is killing me from sitting on the floor while you sat up there on your throne."

"My throne?" Where only a second earlier, she'd been firmly rubbing, she now twinkled her fingers beneath his arms, tickling him senseless.

Rolling over to thwart her attack, he tried tickling her back, but years of practice in escaping her brothers had made her an expert at the arts of both dodging tickles and giving them.

"Okay, okay," he finally yelped, out of breath and laughing. "I surrender."

"And you apologize for that throne comment?"

"Never," he said, a wicked gleam in his eyes.

"Apologize," she said, hitting him with a surprise attack between his ribs.

"All right. You weren't sitting on your throne," he said between laughs. "Just being lazy!"

"Ooh, that's even worse!"

The teasing went back and forth for another five minutes until they were both too exhausted to put up a good fight. Deciding mutual truces would be their best course of action, they collapsed side by side in front of the dancing fire, comfy throw pillows beneath their heads.

"Finn?" Lilly asked after a few minutes of their listening to the rain.

"Yeah?"

"A little while ago, when you mentioned how you nursed me when I was sick?"

"Yeah? What about it?"

"I was wondering," she said, taking a deep breath. "Why did you take such good care of me?" Turning onto her side to face him, she added, "At the time, you hardly knew me."

"You're wrong about that." With his index finger, he lazily reached for her, tracing her eyebrows, cheeks and nose. "I've known you my whole life, Lilly Reilly. I've been waiting for you for as long as I can remember."

"You lost me," she said with a slow smile. "What does that mean?"

Finn was once again on the verge of keeping his most painful experience a secret, but then he saw the warmth in his wife's eyes and decided if she couldn't know the truth about his childhood, then who could? She was the cause of his present happiness. Shouldn't she be let in on the reason he'd previously felt so much pain?

Taking a deep breath, he said, "There's something I haven't told you."

"O-okay..."

"You don't have to look so stricken," he ran his finger along her quivering lower lip. "It's not anything bad—at least not to you. It was to me, but..."

"Whatever it is, tell me. You're scaring me."

He eased himself into an upright position, sitting cross-legged with his back to the fire. "I grew up in this house. When I was a kid, I lived a storybook life. While Dad went off to earn the bacon, Mom cared for my sister and me. The cookie jar was always full of fresh-baked goodies and the kitchen always smelled of home-baked bread."

"That sounds wonderful," she said, her eyes shining with what he prayed might someday be love. "I can't wait to one day meet your parents and sister. Where do they live?"

He swallowed hard. "In heaven."

Still lying on her side, she scrunched up her nose. "Is that in Utah?"

"No, baby," he said, toying with one of her curls. "It's in the clouds."

Realizing his family wasn't a couple hundred miles away, but forever gone, her smile slowly faded. She searched his face for confirmation that what he'd told her was true and when she got it, she scrambled to her knees, only to shuffle the small distance it took to wrap him in her arms. "Oh, Finn. I'm so sorry. What happened? How long has it been since they died?" Waiting for him to answer, she tucked her legs beneath her and sat on her heels.

Finn swallowed years of pent-up grief. "They died when I was eight. I was camping with my scout troop near the mine where I took you. They were on their way to Denver to visit a friend of Mom's who'd had a baby." His words caught in his throat, but still he went on. "They were on Colorado I-70, traveling up Vail Pass when a freak summer snowstorm hit. The storm claimed not just my mom, dad and little sister, but fourteen lives in all. Not thirty minutes after it hit, I've been told that the sun was shining."

"Oh, Finn," she said, taking his hands in hers. "I wish there was something I could do, something I could say."

"But don't you see?" he said, his eyes watering over. "That's what I've been trying not-so-successfully to show you. By agreeing to be my wife, you've already done more than anyone else ever could."

"What do you mean?"

"I mean, my whole life, I've been trying to get back the sense of belonging to a family."

"But you are part of a family. From what I've seen, this whole town loves you."

"I know, and I love them, but as selfish as it sounds, it's not enough. It's never been enough. After my parents died and I had to leave this house to live with my aunt, I always swore I'd come back. I'd fill this house with love the way my parents did for me. I'd bring home a wife who'd sing while she cooked and keep me company on cold winter nights. We'd make lots of beautiful babies and live happily ever after. That's why I fell for you so fast. That's why I knew from what felt like the moment I met you that we were meant to be together, because we were. Angels sent you to me, Lilly.''

Her eyes glowing with warmth and unshed tears, she gave his hands a squeeze. ''Y-you've got that backward,'' she said. ''Angels sent you to me.''

''How's that?''

''Finn…I'm pregnant.''

''You're what?''

''Pregnant. I'm going to have a baby.''

While Finn stared at her for what felt like forever, Lilly's heart pounded. What was he thinking? Why wouldn't he say something? And then, in one crushing hug, he answered her every question.

''Do you have any idea how happy you've made me?'' he asked, drawing her to her feet to hug her all over again. ''This explains so much. Your drinking milk all the time and falling asleep. Reading Rachel's baby book. You didn't have the flu, you had morning sickness. Why didn't you tell me then?''

''I—''

''I know. It happened so fast, it must have been a shock to you, too. Oh, Lilly, this is wonderful. And finding out like this, the day before Thanksgiving.

Now, when I meet your folks for the first time, we'll really have something to celebrate.''

"But, Finn, I—"

"Does Doc Walsh know?"

She nodded.

He lightly smacked himself on the forehead. "No wonder she told me to ask Rachel if we could babysit. She wanted us to practice being a mom and dad."

"So Dr. Walsh told you I was pregnant?"

"No, no," he said, cupping her face with his big hands. "She would never divulge a confidence like that. What she did do was give me a few tips on how to make you fall for me like I already had for you. Showing you I'd make a good father was at the top of her list."

"She's a smart woman," Lilly said, reveling in the arms of this wonderful man. Why hadn't she told Finn about the baby sooner? They could have been this happy for weeks.

"I'll say. Did she have you take a pregnancy test that morning? I mean, we'd only just…you know, that weekend. You couldn't have been more than a few days along."

"Um, yeah." Like curtains rising on a stage, revealing the bad guy at the end of a play, it dawned on Lilly why her husband was taking this news so well.

Finn thinks my baby is his.

"Oh, man," he said, running his fingers through his hair. "This is such a buzz. Like winning the lottery. I can't believe it's finally happened. I'm going to be a dad." After letting out a joyous whoop, he pulled her into his arms, whirling her around and around, kissing her and laughing and making her feel as if, far from her marriage almost being destroyed, it was growing stronger by the second.

Again he was cupping her face with his hands, pressing his lips to hers, sweetly, urgently, begging admittance not only to her heart but her soul. Tears came fast and hot.

Tell him! her conscience cried. *Tell him about Elliot. He'll understand.*

"This also explains all those tears," Finn said, tenderly brushing them away with the pads of his thumbs. "Are these happy tears you're crying now?"

Oh, Finn, think what you're saying. Think back to how I've been this emotional since the moment you first met me. Think of what that implies!

"Babe? Are you okay?" His hands about her waist, he pulled her close for a hug. "Are you still upset about how our relationship began? Are you afraid that because our feelings sprang up so fast they won't stand the test of time?"

She shook her head. "No, I—"

Tell him. Tell him.

"Because if that is the case, it's not true. Think back, Lilly." He lightly pushed her away to look deep into her eyes. "Think back to those first few hours we were together. Our first kiss. Our vows. As much as I tried denying it, I knew even then you were the woman for me. I had that crazy fear you were mixed up with Mitch, but deep down, I knew. I knew angels had handpicked you for me."

"Y-yes, Finn," she said, hardly able to speak through her tears. "Yes. Oh God, yes. I've never wanted anything but you." And she meant it. Lord, how she meant it. It was her turn to explore his face with her hands, the angular planes of his stubbled cheeks and squared set of his jaw and forehead. His deep brown eyes, which never failed to blanket her in security. His eyebrows. His lips. In such a short time, she'd grown hopelessly, wonderfully attached to him. Could this be love? The question terrified her. How many times had she fancied herself in love with Elliot or Dallas, yet look how those relationships had ended.

True, but Finn was different. Finn was infinitely kinder, gentler, all around better.

Through a miraculous twist of fate, he'd become her everything and she couldn't bear to let him go. Not yet. Not when her dreams were so close. She'd tell him the whole truth after Thanksgiving. Then she'd feel strong enough to withstand the pain should he ask her to leave, but until then, she needed time to think. Time to figure out the best way to break his heart by telling him this child wasn't his.

"Make love to me," she sobbed, fisting handfuls of his blue flannel shirt, desperately afraid that if she let go of him for even a second, her house of cards would come tumbling down.

"Are you sure you're ready?" he asked, his voice raspy with tender concern.

She nodded. "I've never been more certain of anything. Make love to me, Finn. I don't want to spend another night outside your arms."

Far from the urgency of the first time they made love, this time, her husband took it agonizingly slow. "I adore you," he said, undoing the buttons one by one on her simple burgundy peasant dress. Though the air by the fire warmed her back, her breasts reacted to the cooler side of the room. Her nipples swelled and hardened as much to the chill as to Finn's appreciative stare. "You're so beautiful," he said, angling her toward the fire, immersing the front half of her body in its radiant glow. "You're everything I've ever dreamed of and now so much more." He drew her dress off her shoulders, smoothing it down until it fell with a whisper to the floor, pooling at her feet.

He lowered himself to his knees, cupping her behind with his big hands while with his mouth he paid homage to her womb. "I'm going to love you so much," he said to the tiny being inside. "You're going to have everything a kid could ever want."

With her husband's every word, Lilly's heart broke more.

After raining soft kisses upon her tummy, then ringing her navel, Finn moved upward, skimming his tongue along the center of her midsection while with his hands he cupped and kneaded her breasts through her scrap of an ivory silk bra.

As his explorations continued ever higher, he swept aside the lace covering her left nipple. He took that hardened bud into his mouth, then the other, drawing with such ardor that all Lilly could do was arch her head in fevered, dizzying pleasure. The heat of the fire and that of her husband's mouth combined, sending velvety chills coursing through her body. She slid her fingers into his hair, holding on with each new havoc he wrought.

Then he was standing, kissing her hard, soft, plundering her with a fervency that set her soul on fire.

Her fingers shy at first, she slipped them in between the buttons of his blue flannel shirt. The fabric was soft, the skin beneath, rock hard and hot. After each button, she planted a kiss to the flesh she'd exposed, and when she reached the bottom, she stretched her arms high, drawing the garment past his shoulders and arms and onto the floor.

She wanted all of him.

Now.

She wanted to skim her palms over his ridges and planes. She wanted to trace her tongue along his abdomen, his nipples, take teasing bites of his beefy shoulders. She wanted to do all that and more, so she did, and when she'd had her fill of his chest, she nimbly unfastened the buttons of his 501s, drawing them down, pooling them on the floor where they caressed her dress at their feet.

Slipping her hands into the waistband of his blue plaid boxers, she slid those down as well, helping her husband lift one foot then the other as she brushed them past his feet.

He stood before her gloriously naked, lit by the fire's hypnotic glow, looking so perfect he could have been carved of stone. "You're the beautiful one," she said, taking the silken steel of him into her hand and giving him a squeeze.

"What are you trying to do to me?" he asked through a groan.

"Make you the happiest man alive."

"Yeah, well, you're succeeding."

She took him into her mouth, wanting to grant him as much pleasure as he'd given her in Vegas. He meant so much. The world. If she never had more than tonight, she wanted it to be perfect.

"Stop," Finn finally said, his fingers in her hair. "It's my turn to have fun."

"I thought you were?" she teased.

"Woman," he said with a playful growl. "You know damn well what I mean." Kicking the clothes aside, he grabbed a colorful quilt from the back of a nearby chair, then tossed it in front of the fire, piling the pillows at one end.

"Care to join me beside the fire, Mrs. Reilly?"

"Mmm, Mr. Reilly, I thought you'd never ask."

He looked at her and frowned.

"What's the matter?"

"You still have your clothes on."

"Not many," she said with a giggle.

"When it comes to you, any clothes are too many."

"Well then, since you've appointed yourself the leader of this expedition, what do you propose I do?"

Pretending to think, he scratched his head. "You could take your bra and panties off."

She defiantly shook her head. "Too simple. I want to see what lengths you're willing to go to have me."

"Hmm," he said, pressing his lips tightly together. "Are you wearing a front- or back-clasping bra?"

She looked down at the scrap of ivory lace. "Back."

"Damn. I was afraid of that. This significantly increases the difficulty of my mission."

"Oh well," she said with a saucy sigh. "If you

haven't been properly trained, I guess I'll have to carry out the mission on my own.'' Reaching behind her, she unhooked the clasp.

"You didn't just do that," he said, his gaze appreciably warming at the sight of her slowly baring her breasts.

Before removing the bra all the way, she said, "I'll put it back on if you'd like?"

Swallowing hard, he said, "Nah…go ahead and finish."

"What if I'm too tired?"

"That's it," he growled, surprising her by snatching the silky scrap and tossing it somewhere behind the sofa. "I've had enough games. Show me your treasure or else…" He'd affected a pirate's brogue and lunged for her, holding her close while ravishing her breasts.

Giggling at his antics, she said, "Pirate Finn, are you *ever* going to make a real woman of me?"

He froze, cocked open one eye. "Is that complaining I hear out of you, ye saucy wench?"

"You'd better believe it. There's a whole burning continent in my southern hemisphere dying to be explored."

"Well, now, we can't have that, can we? Who knows what kind of treasure I might find." He touched her right hip. "Is it here that needs further exploration?"

She shook her head. "Lower."

"Here?" he asked, cupping his open palm over the swell of her tummy.

"Nope." The anticipation of how good it would feel when he finally found the damp, pulsing island between her legs drove her wild. Still he mercilessly played on.

Touching her knee, he said, "This wouldn't happen to be the spot, would it?"

"Higher."

"Here?" He'd reached her inner thigh.

"Higher."

"Here?" He covered the silken mound beneath her panties.

"A tad lower."

"Hmm, to explore that region, as lovely as they are, I'm afraid these panties will have to go." Just as he had in Vegas, he effortlessly ripped the garment at the sides before tossing it.

"I hope you're a rich pirate," she said.

"Why's that?" he asked, urging her legs apart while he spoke directly into the place yearning for his touch. The heat of his breath on her most intimate region had her nearly weeping with need.

"B-because all these panties you keep ripping are expensive."

"Maybe you should stop wearing them." He skimmed his fingers along a particularly hot section of skin. Urging her legs still farther apart, he said, "Because really, what good did that bit of lace do you anyway? It's not as if you need to protect all of this tropical paradise from me. After all, I'm just your everyday, average pirate, doing my best to satisfy my demanding wench."

"Grrr," Lilly said, need driving her close to the edge of sanity. "If you're supposed to be satisfying me, dear sir, then quit yakking and take me to bed!"

LYING IN BED the next morning, light snow falling outside the windows, his wife snuggled beside him, Finn couldn't remember having ever been more content—or exhausted! It had been a wild and wonderful night.

"Woman," he said, toying with one of her blond curls. "You wore me out."

"Are you complaining?" Blue eyes sparkling, she aimed her impish grin straight for his heart.

"Nope. Just stating the facts." After a few minutes of companionable silence, he said, "Tell me again how many brothers and sisters you have?"

"Seven. In descending order from oldest to youngest, David, Kathy, Ben, Mark, Michael, Kristen, Mary, then me."

"Then you? You've got that all wrong. You should have said and finally, wonderfully, you. After you, your parents must have realized they already had the best so why try for any more?"

"Yeah, I never thought of it that way. I've always been kind of the misfit. Getting rotten grades. No interest in college. Never finding a career that fit. All I've ever wanted to do is raise a family."

"Sounds like a noble profession to me."

"Yeah, but you're biased."

"Only because I love you." He planted a soft kiss to her forehead. "Which reminds me, have I told you lately how much you mean to me?"

"Not in at least an hour or so."

"Then it's time for an update. Let's see, I've already told you how much I adore your lush little body."

She playfully rolled her eyes. "Only about a dozen times."

"And I've expressed my excitement for our bundle of joy," he said, smoothing his warm hand over her tummy.

"That was about two dozen times."

"Can't be. I've only been playing this game since midnight."

"Mmm," she said, snuggling close, her naked body pressed to his beneath the heavy down comforter. "And what a fun game it's been."

"Hush, woman. I'm trying to think of a new way that I love you besides the physical."

Her stomach growled. Looking toward that region, she said, "I've got a great appetite."

"True, but I'm looking for something splashy."

"How about the fact that if you'd let me out of this bed, I could whip us up a couple of mean cheeseburgers?"

"Nope. I've got it. I know I've told you this before," he said, combing stray curls from her blue eyes, "but this is so good, it bears repeating."

"In that case, I'm all ears."

"Actually, you're all smart mouth. Where was I?"

"Singing my praises."

"Oh yeah. All joking aside, one of my favorite things about you is knowing how incredibly principled you are."

"Finn, I—"

"No," he said, pressing his fingertips softly to her lips. "Let me say this. After what Vivian did to me, I never thought I'd trust a woman again, but you've proved that not all women are out to work their own agendas. With you, I know that you're every bit as devoted to me as I am to you. I know that you're not going to lie to me or play silly head games. You're too good for that kind of childish nonsense. In short, you're perfect.'' He ended his speech by drawing her into a deep kiss.

What Finn hadn't admitted was just how grateful he was to have found such an on-the-level woman. He'd been hurt so many times in his life, he didn't think he could live through it were someone to hurt him again. But then what was he thinking? Here it was Thanksgiving Day. He was about to meet more family than even he'd imagined having. Not only would he have his wife by his side, but his growing child. Life didn't get any better.

Even though it was snowing outside, for once in a very long time, Finn Reilly had nothing but sunshine in his heart. And after twenty-five years of eternal winter, spending the rest of his days bathed in Lilly's warmth was exactly where he wanted to be.

Chapter Thirteen

Lilly stared out the truck's window, watching Mother Nature transform the usually brown landscape alongside I-15 into a winter wonderland. This should have been one of the happiest days of her life, ranking right up there with her wedding day, but the daunting task she had ahead of her in telling Finn about Elliot being the real father of her baby scared her to the core.

Even worse, since Elliot's parents were friends with hers, what if she ran into him? What would he think of her all of the sudden being married? Would he suspect she'd married for a reason? If he did, he surely wouldn't tell anyone what that reason was, would he? After all, he had as much to lose by blabbing about their brief relationship as she did.

Squeezing her eyes shut, Lilly tried clearing her mind of anything but how delicious her mother's meal would taste and how good it would be to once again chat with her siblings. Even if they were perfect, she loved them.

"You're awfully quiet over there," Finn said from behind the wheel. "Quarter for your thoughts."

"A quarter, huh?" She flashed him a grin. "I doubt they're worth that much."

"Try me."

Shifting on the bench seat to face him, she said, "For the first time ever, I'm finally on an even keel with my brothers and sisters."

"How so?"

"I'm married to a wonderful husband, have a baby on the way. I've quit my job at the bookstore that they always secretly thought was beneath me."

"How do you know that's what they thought? To my way of thinking, you had a job and were making your own way in the world. Even better, it was a job that allowed you to live life on your own terms. You had plenty of time to read. No stress. All in all, it seems like a pretty great gig to me."

"But not to my family. David—the oldest, is a marriage counselor with at least ten degrees after his name. Kathy's been married forever. She has a high-profile accounting job, four great kids and is head of the PTA, both Boy and Girl Scout troops, teaches Sunday school and still manages to keep an immaculate house. Ben is an award-winning policeman. He has a sweet wife who runs a needlepoint store and raises twin daughters. Mark is a lawyer. His wife is a judge and their son just won—"

"Okay, okay, I get the picture. Your family sounds pretty daunting, but then look at all your accomplishments."

She raised her eyebrows. "Mind telling me what those might be?"

"You caught me, didn't you?" Reaching for her hand, he gave it a quick kiss.

"Yeah, but the only reason I caught you is so you could save your truck. Face it, Finn, you married an only recently reformed misfit."

After scowling her way, he steered the truck onto the paved shoulder, then moved the gearshift to park.

Her purse slipped from the seat to the floor and, while picking up everything from keys to lipstick to her wallet, she asked, "What's wrong? Did we have a blowout? Was there an animal in the road?"

"None of the above." Setting the emergency brake, he unfastened his seat belt and turned to face her. "The only emergency here is the state of your self-esteem."

"I'm all right," she said. "Really, sometimes I just get a twinge impatient for my own life to start. I want to show off my baby pictures and ribbons my cookies won at the county fair." *And I'm terrified that once we get home and I tell you the truth about Elliot being the father of my baby you'll never speak to me again. All these dreams of mine that are finally within reach will go poof, back to the realm of fairy tales that failed to come true.*

"You'll do all of those things you want and so much more, Lilly. Give it time. You're young. How much older are these paragons of accomplishment you keep raving about?"

Sniffing back tears, she said, "David's eighteen years older than me."

"Well, there you go," Finn said with a laugh, pulling her close. "I would hope he'd have accomplished something in all that time. You have your whole life ahead of you to have babies, be my wife, work at a job you love. Don't you see? Now that we've found each other, anything's possible. All we have to do is dream it and it's ours.''

Trying harder than ever to hold back tears, Lilly painfully added to her thoughts. *Does that mean if I wish hard enough, you'll not only forgive me for hiding the truth about my child from you, but accept him or her as your own?*

GAZING DOWN THE LENGTH of the cloth-covered plywood-and-sawhorse table lined with loving, laughing, family—*his* family, a feeling of bone-deep satisfaction filled Finn's soul. Lilly had been right. Her mom and dad, brothers, sisters and in-laws were amazing people. The majority of them had Lilly's blond hair and rosy cheeks—even her bold blue eyes. His dark hair and sudden appearance clearly should have set him apart as a stranger to this boisterous crowd, but nothing could have been further from the truth. From the moment his wife introduced him, they'd welcomed him as if they'd known him their whole lives.

The rich scents of turkey and ham, mashed potatoes, sweet potatoes, gravy and buttered rolls all mingled together, reminding him how hungry he was and how the coming feast would be the first Thanksgiving that hadn't felt empty since the death of his own family.

Swallowing hard, he prayed, *Mom, Dad, Sis...thank you. Somewhere up there, I know you're smiling down on me. Though no family could ever replace the love*

I feel for all of you, finally, I feel as if I've found another home.

Finn's father-in-law clanged his fork against his wineglass, then, from his seat beside Lilly's mom at the head of the table, he stood. "Before we eat this magnificent meal, I'd like to say a few words."

Good-natured groans abounded.

Midway down the table set for nearly thirty, Lilly's brother David said, "Be quick, Dad. Mark's got his eye on the drumstick."

"Luckily, the good Lord saw fit to put two legs on that bird, which means you have no reason not to sit there and listen to every word I say."

Turning to his daughter and Finn, he said, "Lilly, I've always been especially fond of you—not that I don't love every single one of my brood, but you're my baby, and as such, you will always hold a special place in my heart."

"Aw," Lilly's sister, Mary, said from the seat beside her, eyes shining with unshed tears. "You're my baby, too."

Lilly's mom, nodding, placed her hand on her husband's arm.

"Okay, so I'm assuming it's fairly safe to say that we all feel extra special about our little Lilly who's not so little anymore."

"Here, here," David said, raising his glass high. "To Baby Lilly!"

"To Baby Lilly!" everyone cheered.

"I'm not finished yet," her dad complained, "but what the heck, this toast'll be a warm up. To Baby Lilly!"

While some laughed, others openly shed happy tears.

"Okay then, where I was headed with this, I have no idea. I just wanted to say how pleased I am for you, sweetheart. I'm still peeved about missing my chance to walk you down the aisle, but your mother assures me that if your wedding day was special for the two of you, then that's all that matters."

"Here, here," David said, "Let's toast Baby Lilly's marriage."

Lilly's dad shot his son a look.

"What can I say? I'm hungry?"

While everyone else laughed, David's wife gave him a good-natured whack.

"In conclusion—"

"Grandpa Tom," piped Mary's daughter, three-year-old Erin. "You talk too much!"

"All right," Grandpa Tom said, a twinkle in his blue eyes—Lilly's blue eyes. "I get the message." Raising his glass one final time, he said, "Here's to Finn Reilly, the newest member of our family and hearts. May you and our little girl live happily ever after!"

"To happily ever after!"

Lilly's mom said a blessing for the food, then all pandemonium broke out in a mad grab for grub.

"Um, I know you're all hungry," Finn said above the clang of serving forks and spoons, "but I do have one more quick announcement—and I do mean quick."

"Go ahead," Tom said, a bite of turkey poised at his lips. "But we're going to hold you to your promise to be quick. Mother, here, makes the best turkey around and I've been waiting since last Thanksgiving for another taste.''

"No offense to your cooking, Mrs. Churchill, but since my wife here has been shy on this matter, I thought I'd go ahead and tell you the news myself.''

Lilly dropped her fork to her plate. *No! Finn, don't tell them I'm pregnant. If they don't know, then there won't be any way of Elliot knowing, either.*

Standing, wrapping his arm around Lilly's shoulder and giving her a squeeze, he said proudly, "Your daughter and I are already expecting.''

All food forgotten, Lilly was stampeded by hugs and well wishes. While her mother burst into joyful tears, her sisters began planning a baby shower and her brothers patted Finn on his back.

While she should have told them all right then and there the truth about the baby, the look of pride on her husband's face was too precious to publicly shatter. She'd tell him the truth the second they got home. Until then, not only would she let him revel in this moment, but she'd indulge in a small slice of happiness, as well.

All her life, she'd celebrated her siblings joys, but now, finally, it was her turn to be lauded. What could it hurt to hold on to her secret a short while longer?

"HE'S A HUNK," Lilly's sister Mary said an hour later, scrubbing a rose-adorned plate, then passing it to Lilly to rinse while her sister Kathy dried.

David's wife, Stacie, hard at work on leftover disbursement at the kitchen's center island said, ''And did you ever see such broad shoulders?'' Closing her eyes, she sighed. ''He's like Jean-Claude Van Damme and Tom Cruise all rolled into one. Mmm, your baby is going to be adorable.''

''Would you guys knock it off,'' Lilly said.

''What's the matter with you, squirt?'' Mary flicked her sister with bubbles. ''We're all happily married. What's it hurt to let us dream about your guy for a while instead of our flabby couch potatoes?''

''Speak for yourself,'' Heather, the policeman's wife, said. ''Ben is buff.''

''That's true,'' Mary conceded. ''But the rest of our guys could use a couple years' worth of workouts.''

''Mary,'' Lilly's mom said, stepping in from the living room to supervise the cleanup. ''That's enough yammering about how cute Finn is, although—'' she looked over her shoulder to see if any of the guys had followed her into the room ''—he is a real stud, isn't he?''

''Mom!'' Lilly's cheeks pinkened in horror. ''Where did you even learn the word *stud?*''

''I know all kinds of words,'' she said with a wink. ''In fact, just the other day your father and I were making out when he said I was a—''

''No!'' Mary cried. ''No more sharing of Dad's and your sex lives. I can't take it anymore.''

''Why not? I should think you'd be glad that your father and I still lust for each other.''

''We are, Mom,'' Stacie said from her center-island post, wrapping the turkey tray with foil. ''We just don't want to hear about it.''

''Yeah,'' concurred the rest of the women.

Mary said, "It's kind of depressing to know your mother gets more action than you do."

"Speak for yourself." Lilly's grin was wide. "Last night was pretty amazing."

Mary was back to flicking suds.

"Hey!" Lilly cried. "Can I help it if, like Mom said, I married a stud?"

"You just wait," Stacie said. "Before you know it, your baby will be here and then you and that stud muffin of yours can kiss your intimate nights good-bye."

Mary washed the last plate, then handed it to Lilly. "You know," she said, "I used to be so envious of you. Frittering away your time in that quaint book-store, dating, doing whatever you wanted with your time. But now, you're just like the rest of us, little sis. Welcome to the grown-up club."

Mary, envious of her? "In case you haven't noticed, I've been a grown-up for quite some time now."

"Yeah," Stacie said, sliding a bowl of cranberries into the fridge. "But you've been a grown-up without all the hassles. No orthodontists, no surprise plumbing bills."

"No cooking for last-minute business parties," added Janine, Michael's wife.

"But don't you see?" Lilly said. "I've been envious of what all of you have. You all lead the perfect lives and I've just been sitting at home, night after night."

"Poor Lilly," Mary said. "Soaking for uninterrupted hours up to her neck in hot bubbles."

Stacie added, "Not having to share the remote."

"Jeez, guys," Lilly said, drying a china gravy boat. "You're scaring me. Is married life that much drudgery?"

"Don't you listen to them, baby." Her mother gave her a quick hug from behind. "Married life has its ups and downs. Believe you me, there have been plenty of times I've felt like sending your dad packing, but looking back over the years, I wouldn't have traded a second. It's those moments late at night, when the kids are finally asleep—or blessedly moved out of the house—and you're lying on cold sheets and find those warm, familiar arms reaching out to draw you close. That's when you truly appreciate marriage. Well, that and the fact that having a man around means you don't have to take out the trash."

"Oh, Mom!" Laughing, Stacie playfully threw a dishrag at the older woman. "And here I thought you were about to impart some genuine pearls of wisdom."

"I did. I can't help it if you don't hold the proper appreciation for what it'd be like to haul out your own trash." She plucked the dishrag from the floor and slipped into the utility room to toss it into the washer. "Anyway, what I originally came in here for was to hurry you along. The Dinsmoores have invited us over for cookies and caroling at six and I don't want to be late."

Crash.

Lilly's great-great-great-grandmother's china gravy boat—the one that had been brought to Utah in a covered wagon all the way from Boston—slipped from her hands, shattering on the hardwood floor.

"Lilly!" her mom called out, rushing to her side. "What's the matter with you? All of the sudden you look white as a ghost."

"I'm sorry about the dish, Mom. I didn't mean to break it." Kneeling, she began the heartrending process of picking up the larger pieces of china. How could she have been so careless? That dish was an heirloom she could have passed on to her daughter. Yet again, Lilly felt like the family misfit. This time, because of Elliot. She couldn't go to his parents for caroling. She wouldn't.

"Here, let me do that," Mary said. "You go lie down."

"I don't want to lie down," Lilly said. "This is my mess, I'll clean it."

Mary backed away. "Was it something we said that has you upset? We were kidding about all those bad points of marriage, you know. I wouldn't trade Robby for anything."

That's just it, Lilly's heart cried. *You would never have to because your marriage is based upon truth. Mine, however, is built upon nothing but lies. Lies that if Elliot is at his parent's house tonight could blow up in my face.*

Still picking at the china, Lilly said, "I'm not going."

"Why?" her mother asked, her voice laced with concern. "You love the Dinsmoores. They've always been like a second family to you."

"I don't feel good." Putting her hand to her pounding forehead, Lilly stood.

"Nonsense," her mother said. "A second ago you

told us you felt fine. Now I don't know what's the matter with you all of the sudden, but caroling with the Dinsmoores is a family tradition.''

"Yeah," Lilly fought. "One we usually don't participate in until a couple weeks before Christmas.''

"Lillian Diane Churchill-Reilly. You're going to the Dinsmoores for caroling and that's final.''

Chapter Fourteen

In the Dinsmoores crowded, two-story entry hall, Finn leaned close to Lilly and whispered, "Who are all these people again?"

"Remember back in Vegas when I told you about Elliot? The guy who played me for a fool?"

"Yeah?"

"Rose and Harold Dinsmoore are his parents."

"Is he going to be here?"

I hope not! A few more neighbors entered the cramped space, forcing Finn and Lilly against the oak stair railing. Mrs. Dinsmoore had already put up her Christmas decorations and the fragrant pine boughs wrapping the newel post stabbed Lilly's behind. Stepping a few inches away from the prickly decor, she said, "Probably Elliot won't be here. He got married not too long ago, so most likely he's at his wife's family's house."

"I hope he *is* here. I'd like to sock him in the gut for what he did to you."

As perversely pleased as she was at the thought of Finn beating the tar out of Elliot, Lilly said, "Whoa, there, fella. You might want to tone down the testosterone.''

"Why? He hurt you.''

"Yeah, but I was stupid enough to let him.''

He sighed. "You're completely missing my point. Anyway, how long do we have to stay? I was kind of hoping to try out that old twin bed of yours.''

"Finn!" she muttered under her breath, blushing furiously at the thought of what the two of them could do in that teeny-tiny bed.

"What?'' he whispered back. "Are you telling me you don't think it might be fun to see how quiet we can be while at the same time seeing how bad we can be?''

"Grrr, what I'm saying is—''

"There's my pretty Lilly.'' Elliot's mom, Rose, called out, easing her way through the crowd to pull Lilly into a hug. "When Elliot married Missy, I thought my heart would break. She's a lovely girl, but you know I always had my hopes set on my boy marrying you. You two could have raised my grandbabies right next door.''

Lilly flashed her a weak smile. "You know what folks say about things having a way of working themselves out for the best.''

"I suppose, but I still say you would have made the perfect daughter-in-law. So,'' she said, eyeing Finn, "is this that handsome husband of yours your mother told me about?''

"He sure is,'' Lilly said, growing more relaxed by the minute. Surely if Elliot was in the house, Rose wouldn't have dissed his choice in wives? "Mrs. Dinsmoore, meet my husband, Finn Reilly."

"Reilly," she said, pursing her lips into a frown. "I knew some Reillys who went to the Presbyterian church on Maple. Are you any relation?"

"No, ma'am, 'fraid not," Finn said, warmly shaking her hand.

"That's a relief. I never did care for Helen Reilly. She made this horrible sucking noise through her dentures. Like to drove me batty during our women's prayer meetings. Anywho, it's nice meeting you, Finn." She gave his shoulder an affectionate pat. "You two young people go mingle. Elliot and Missy are around here somewhere."

Lilly's heart stopped, then started up again, racing at an unfathomable pace.

"Hon? Are you okay?" Finn asked.

"Yes, I—no. I think I need some fresh air. I—" The space was so cramped and the smells of spiced cider and cinnamon potpourri and fresh pine cuttings combined to bring on an even fiercer headache than she'd had earlier while washing dishes.

"Rose?" Lilly's mom called out. "Did my daughter and new son tell you their joyous news?"

"No?" Rose said, her thin eyebrows arched high. "Don't tell me? You two aren't expecting, too?"

"You'd better believe it," Finn said, snugly wrapping his arm around Lilly's waist. "No messing around for us. We both wanted to start a family right away, and bam—that's exactly what happened."

"How wonderful," Rose said. "Wait right here

while I go get Elliot and Missy. They're expecting, too, you know."

"I need to go," Lilly said to Finn, clutching his arm. "All these people. The heat."

"Let's stay a minute longer," he said. "I want to get a load of this chump Elliot's reaction when he hears you're already carrying my baby."

"Finn," she tried warning. "I don't think that's such a good idea. We should—"

"Lookee who I found," Rose sang out. "Elliot, hurry. It's your old flame, Lilly Churchill, from next door. And look how much prettier she is with that expectant glow of a new mom."

The look Elliot cast Lilly could have frozen over hell. "Congratulations," he said. "Mom, told me you'd recently gotten hitched. Is this the lucky guy?"

"I sure am," Finn said, holding out his hand for Elliot to shake. "We've been married almost a month now and neither of us have ever been happier."

"That's real niii-ce," Elliot said, his voice squeaking when Finn shook his hand.

Lilly cringed. Finn, almost a full head taller than Elliot must have shaken her former beau's hand harder than necessary. Still, so far so good. Despite the fact that her heart felt ready to pound right out of her chest, Lilly took Elliot's chilly demeanor as a sign that he too was reluctant for anyone to discover their affair.

The day would come when she'd have to tell him her baby was his, but if everything went as planned, she wouldn't be telling Elliot until *after* she told her husband.

"GATHER AROUND, everyone!" Rose called from in front of a crackling fire.

Trying desperately to pretend she didn't even know Elliot, let alone that he was standing a mere ten feet away, Lilly put on a brave smile and snuggled closer to her husband. At the rear of the room, they shared a cozy padded bench.

"I hope we do 'Silent Night,'" Finn said. "Mom used to sing that in our church choir and every year her solo blew the congregation away." Wrapping his arm about Lilly's shoulders, he said, "Have you ever sung in a choir?"

Her throat tight, thinking of the heartsick boy her husband must have been when he'd lost his whole family at such a young age, she shook her head. Now was hardly the time to tell him she'd been blackballed from her church's third-grade choir for gluing the hymnal pages together of the songs she didn't like.

"You should, you know. You have a beautiful voice."

"Thank you." His compliment warmed her like a steamy mug of cocoa.

"You're welcome."

With Finn's arm still around her, making her brave, Lilly gazed across the room at the way Elliot affectionately nuzzled his wife's neck. The pretty brunette cast him a smile of pure devotion, and it sickened Lilly to know that not only could her own marriage be blown apart by news of her baby's parentage, but Missy's, as well.

Rose started off the caroling with a rousing rendition of "Jingle Bells" and finally Lilly relaxed. Elliot no more wanted to make a scene than she did. Besides, what motive would he have? He didn't even know her baby was his.

"I love you," Finn whispered in her ear at the end of the song. "This is nice."

"Caroling?"

"Yeah. You forget, it's been a while since I've done something like this. Sure, I usually throw a big Christmas bash for my construction crew down at Lu's, but somehow drinking beer with the guys while singing 'Rudolph the Drunken Reindeer' isn't the same."

"I'm glad you're having fun," she said, her tone perhaps too heartfelt. Lowering her gaze, she said, "That's all I want, Finn, is for you to always be happy."

"Hey," he tilted her chin, forcing her to meet his gaze. "You okay?"

"I'm fine. Just tired and a little thirsty. Mind if I sit this next song out in the kitchen?"

"Nope. In fact, now that you mention it, I'll come with you. I could use some punch."

"Okay, everyone," Rose called out. "It's time for 'Silent Night!'"

As Lilly stood, Finn gazed her way. "I'll meet you in a sec," he said. "I'd love to sing along to this one. You know, for old time's sake."

"Want me to stay?"

"Nah, you go on ahead." His eyes looked suspiciously full. "I'd like to do this on my own. Take a second to give thanks for you and our baby coming into my life."

"O-okay," she said, even though the heavy ache in her chest was anything but okay.

She quickly slipped from the room, hoping no one noticed her using the backs of her hands to wipe away sentimental tears. She was so happy it hurt.

The kitchen was blessedly quiet and looked much the same as it had when she'd played there as a child. Mrs. Dinsmoore took pride in her baked goods and every day after school, while Elliot and Lilly played board games or watched cartoons, she presented them with trays of cookies or blueberry muffins.

"Do you mind if I have a word with you, Lilly?"

She spun around. "Elliot," she said, putting her hand to her chest. "You startled me. I didn't hear you come in."

"I startled you?" he said. "Ha! That's rich. Come on, we need to talk." Casting a wary gaze over his shoulder, he pulled her into his mother's king-size pantry, flicked on the dim light and shut the door. Inside, the air smelled of flour and nutmeg and a multitude of other homey spices that felt out of sync with Lilly's pensive mood.

"What do you want?" she whispered. "Because as far as I'm concerned, we have nothing more to say."

"The hell we don't." Even through her heavy red sweater, his hold on the soft skin of her upper arm hurt. "For starters, why are you here?"

She raised her chin. "To visit my parents. Is that a crime?"

"Not at all. I just don't want you getting any ideas in your head about telling my wife about our affair."

"*Our* affair?" She laughed. "Correction. Make that

your affair. I had no idea you were married. I was horrified. And once I discovered I was preg—'' Her hand flew to her mouth.

Tightening his grip on her arm, he said, ''Are you telling me the baby you're carrying is mine?''

Dizzy. Hot. Nauseous. The words didn't come close to describing the anguish gripping her body. What had she done?

''Answer me, Lilly.'' From the living room came the faint voices of their family and friends starting ''Deck the Halls.'' ''Is your baby mine?''

''Yes, but—''

''Damn,'' he said, letting loose of her to pound his fist against the wall.

Lilly jumped.

The force of his blow rattled the neat row of home-made pickles lining the shelf behind him.

''This isn't good. Not good at all.'' Eyeing her, he said, ''You're not expecting me to play a part in this kid's life, are you?''

''No, in fact, I—''

''That's good. Damned good. I don't even know how I'm going to support my own kid, let alone yours.''

Bravely swallowing back tears, Lilly said, ''That's fine with me, Elliot. As far as I'm concerned, my husband will be this child's father in every sense of the word.''

''So he knows the kid isn't his?''

''No, but—''

Elliot clutched his stomach, laughing. ''You married that guy because you were pregnant and needed a father for your baby, didn't you? Priceless, Lil. This is priceless." Slapping her on her back, he said, "I always knew you were a resourceful gal, but this beats all. You're nothing but a con artist with an angel's face."

"Elliot, I—" She started to tremble, and silent tears streamed down her cheeks. She had to get away from this man. This place.

"Quit the innocent act. As sure as I'm standing here, you purposely duped this guy, didn't you?"

"No. He means the world to me and believe me, more than anything, I wish this baby was his."

"Right," he said with a cruel snort. "And I'm the pope. So? When were you planning on springing this news on my wife?"

"Never."

"You're damned right," he said, gripping her arm again and squeezing harder than ever. "She *never* needs to know any of this. What the two of us shared was for fun and if you had any experience at all, you'd have been on the pill."

"Stop," Lilly sobbed.

"Oh, I'll stop all right, as soon as you get it through your head that I don't want to see you or this kid ever again."

"Okay," she said. "Just go. Leave me alone."

"My pleasure." After giving her a mock salute, he mercifully left.

Finn. She needed him. His strength, his warmth.

Never would she have guessed Elliot had the capacity to be so cruel.

Quivering with relief that the ugly scene was over,

her legs felt like soft sticks of butter. Yet as hurtful as Elliot's words had been, they could have been so much worse had Finn overheard. What she needed to do, Lilly thought, smoothing her hair and dress as if bringing order to her appearance would bring order to her mind, was calm down. Just because Elliot was upset didn't mean she had to be. His outburst had had no affect on her plan to tell Finn everything as soon as they got home.

She knew her husband better than she'd ever known anyone. He had to understand about her baby. He had to. She couldn't survive if he didn't.

Forcing her breathing to slow, she reached into a plastic sack of red Santa napkins, drawing one out to use as a tissue.

Everything will be all right.
Everything will be all right.

In preparation for blending back into the crowd, she took a deep breath. If Finn asked why she looked as if she'd been crying, she'd say she'd been caught up in the holiday spirit.

Hand poised on the pantry's doorknob, she reminded herself that she was strong. After what had just happened, she could handle anything. She was no longer Lilly Churchill—misfit, but Lilly Reilly. Strong, intelligent woman. Fully capable of cleaning up her own messes.

Spirits bolstered, she straightened her shoulders, threw open the door and marched right out of the pantry and into her husband. "Finn! You startled me."

"I'm sure I did."

She wrapped her arms around him, hugging him

tight. He felt so good, but why was he stiff? Holding his arms to his sides instead of returning her hug. "How was the song?" she asked. "Did it sound as good as you remembered?"

"No."

"Why not?"

"Probably because I wasn't listening."

"Oh?" What was wrong? He'd steeled his jaw and his eyes looked cold instead of filled with their usual warmth. "I thought you were looking forward to singing along."

"I was, but I was worried about you. That's why I came into the kitchen instead of singing. When I heard raised voices, I started to leave. I figured a personal altercation wasn't any of my business. But then I heard your name and I realized what was being discussed was very much my business, wasn't it, Lilly?"

The room spun.

Her blood ran hot and cold.

Dear God, no. Please, God, don't let Finn have heard.

She licked her lips. Fought for air. "Finn, I—I can explain."

"I'm sure you can," he said, his voice icy and expression not much warmer. "The problem is, I'm no longer interested in anything you have to say."

"Y-you don't mean that," she said, searching his face for any sign of forgiveness. "I know you, Finn. I know you'll understand." She reached for his hand, for his reassurance, but he jerked away.

"I'm sure that's exactly what you'd like to believe, isn't it? Good old trustworthy Finn. He'll buy your story hook, line and sinker. He's so desperate for a kid, he'll take in anybody's baby.'' Grasping her firmly by the shoulders, he gave her a slight shake. "Lies, Lilly. Every single damn thing we've ever shared has been nothing but a lie, hasn't it?''

"No, Finn,'' she said, sobbing into his chest. "It wasn't like that. If you'd just listen. Let me explain.'' She clung to him, fisting his shirt. "Let's go back to my parents' house. It'll be quiet there and we can talk. I was planning to tell you all of this on Monday. I wanted to wait until we got home. I thought this was something better discussed in private.''

"Sure.'' He let out a short, sharp laugh before turning down the dark hall leading to the back door. "You were going to tell me Monday, huh? That's easy to say now that the damage is done.''

"Please, Finn,'' she begged, throwing herself against him, trying futilely to make him understand. "Take me with you. We'll go home to Greenleaf tonight. We'll leave my parents a note.''

"Don't touch me,'' he said from between clenched teeth, pushing her away. "I'm leaving all right, but you're not coming with. As far as I'm concerned, as of this moment, you're a stranger to me, Lilly. I wish I'd never met you and I sure as hell never want to see you again.''

FOR THE LONGEST TIME after Finn left, Lilly stood in the cold, dark hall doing what she didn't know. Waiting for Finn to come running back to apologize for the hurtful things he'd said? Then it occurred to her that she was the one who'd hurt him. If anyone had apologizing to do, it was her.

And so she swallowed what tiny bit was left of her pride and ran after her husband, oblivious to her family and friends singing a rowdy "We Wish You a Merry Christmas." Unless she somehow made her husband understand she never meant to hurt him, Lilly feared she might never have another merry Christmas.

Without her coat, oblivious to the biting wind, she ran across her parents' snow-covered yard. All that mattered was Finn. Would she reach him in time to beg him to take her with him?

Bursting through the front door, her mind and body filled with renewed hope, she cried, "Finn? Finn, are you still here?" She received no reply, but that didn't necessarily mean anything. He could be upstairs, packing.

Chasing up the winding staircase she'd sledded down as a kid, she now only had adult matters on her mind. Matters like how to save her marriage.

"Finn? Sweetie? Are you up here?" At the top of the stairs, she raced for her bedroom, knowing he'd still be there, and thankfully, just as she'd prayed, he was.

After shoving the rest of his clothes into his duffel bag and zipping it shut, he looked up. His eyes were red. "I told you back at the Dinsmoores that we have nothing more to discuss."

"How can you say that? We have everything to discuss. I can't believe it took me this long to realize it, Finn, but I love you. Please don't let Elliot's few words change your entire outlook on what we've worked so hard to build.''

"Have *we* worked hard, Lilly? Because I don't see it that way. Looking back on it, I spent this past month doing everything in my power to atone for making you the object of a bet. Only the joke was really on me, wasn't it? Because you'd been playing me all along. From the night you strolled into Lu's looking for a husband, you didn't give a damn who that husband was, just that he'd make a good father for Elliot's child. You knew Elliot wanted to stay with his wife, so unless you wanted your baby born a bastard, you had no option but to get married. That's why you didn't want a divorce back in Vegas—not because of some deeply felt moral convictions about once a man and woman sleep together they're bound forever, but because plain and simple, you'd found a daddy for baby and a provider for you, and you weren't about to give up that meal ticket.''

Tears streaming down her cheeks, she went to him. "Oh, no, Finn. How could you think that? When I thought I was marrying Dallas, he knew he was getting not just a wife but a child. After we married and you never brought up my baby, I thought you'd changed your mind about raising another man's child.'' Wringing her hands, she said, "And then, when I found out you weren't Dallas, I was afraid you never wanted to have kids. But then we got to Greenleaf and I saw how wonderful you were with Chrissy and Randy and Abby. Can't you see? I've grown to love you, Finn. Not because you could give me and my baby a nice house, but because you're you.'' Her hand to his dear, familiar cheek, she said, "I love you. Maybe I've always loved you. That's why I had such a hard time telling you the truth about the baby, because I was terrified of how you'd take the news. And see? Your reaction is proving me right. You don't love me enough to raise another man's child. I knew it all along."

"No, Lilly," he said, snatching his bag from the bed and heading for the door. "I would have gladly accepted both you and this child for the miracle you both were if only from the beginning you'd told me the truth. As it is, I don't know whether you're the woman I married or another coldhearted creature like Vivian who never really loved me at all, but thought of me as a good time. And again, just like Vivian, you played me for a fool not just in private, but in front of family and friends—people I instantly cared for as much as you. Do you know how that makes me feel, Lilly? Do you have any idea what a jackass I must have looked like playing the role of proud papa when you knew all along I wasn't your baby's real father?"

"Please forgive me," Lilly said, following him to the door. "Take me home with you. We can talk about all of this on the ride back."

"Not a chance. Fool me once, shame on you. Fool me twice, shame on me." Aiming his index finger at her chest, his hard stare boring into hers, he said, "It's time for me to grow up. I'm not the eight-year-old boy who lost his parents anymore. I'm a flesh-and-blood man who offered you everything any woman could ever dream of on a silver platter. The absolute only thing I asked of you was to be straight with me, yet you couldn't do even that. Well, now I'll be straight with you. Starting right here, right now, our marriage is over.''

Chapter Fifteen

"What are you doing?" Lilly's sister Mary asked an hour later, seeing Lilly lugging her suitcase down the stairs. "I noticed you'd left the caroling party and when I couldn't find Finn, either, Mom sent me to check on you."

"Something awful's happened, Mary, but I don't have time to explain. Can I borrow your car?"

"Why? It's nearly ten o'clock and the roads are a mess. And where's Finn? He's not ill, is he?"

"Not in the way you mean." Lilly tugged her bag the rest of the way down the stairs.

Hands on her hips, Mary said, "Then tell me how."

"We had a fight, okay? Now, can you give me the keys to your car, or should I take Mom's car?"

"Neither," Mary said, blocking Lilly's path to the door. "You're not going anywhere until you tell me what's going on. I mean, I know newlyweds fight, but one minute you two couldn't keep your eyes and hands off each other and the next he's left you here with him chasing off to God only knows where?"

"Mary, please, just let me go."

"No." Softening her voice, she said, "Let me fix

you a cup of tea. Once you tell me why you need my car, if I deem it necessary, I'll ask Mom to watch the kids and Robby and I will drive you wherever you want to go, but first you have to tell me why.''

Thirty minutes later, seated at the long pine kitchen table, just as they had years earlier when discussing dating problems, Lilly spilled all to her big sister. The *whole* story, starting from how Elliot had taken her virginity to how desperately she'd grown to love Finn, to how terrified she was of never again earning his trust.

A dozen hugs and three mugs of tea later, Mary said, ''Oh, honey, you have gotten yourself into one heck of a jam, but you know what?''

Lilly shook her head.

''I don't care what he says, Finn loves you. He can deny it all he wants, but I saw the way he looks at you. He's lost, down for the count, and the only woman who can bring him back into this fight we call life is you.''

''Exactly,'' Lilly said, ''which is why I have to go to him tonight. To make him understand that I kept the truth from him not out of a desire to hurt him, but out of a selfish desire not to hurt myself.''

Mary sighed. ''Look, you may not want to hear this, but I'm going to say it anyway. You've botched this situation from the start. From the instant you found out you were pregnant, instead of developing some harebrained scheme to marry this Dallas guy you'd only met through e-mails, why didn't you come to us for help? You know how much we love you, Lilly. We're your family. We'd do anything for you.''

''But that's just it. All my life, you've been bailing me out of jam after jam, but after this, I thought for sure Mom and Dad would disown me. I mean, isn't it about time I grew up and learned how to save myself? If only Elliot hadn't confronted me, I'd have had this all worked out.''

''You think so, huh? You've been sitting on a potential powder keg for weeks, and you think that's *worked out?*''

''No.'' Lilly glanced at her watch. ''Which is again the reason why I have to go to Finn—now.''

''You're not going anywhere,'' Mary said with renewed conviction. ''As for your fear of our parents disowning you—that's just plain silly. And I don't blame Finn for being upset. What he found out purely by accident tonight must have been one heck of a blow to his pride. What he needs is time to come around. If he truly loves you…as I believe with all my heart he does, he'll be back.''

''DAMMIT, PETE, if I'd wanted this bathtub green, I'd have ordered it that way.'' A week before Christmas, Finn looked at the offensive special-order whirlpool tub that was going to cost him at least a thousand bucks in lost labor and shipping fees to send back to the manufacturer and felt like kicking it.

''Yeah, but, boss—''

''I don't wanna hear excuses, just rip the damn thing out and get a white one ordered ASAP.''

''But, boss—''

''For cryin' out loud, Pete.'' Finn slashed his fingers

through his hair. "Just do it. I don't have the patience for this kind of amateur screwup."

His plumber for the past seven years stormed off, mumbling a string of curses that'd make a sailor proud.

The morning was so cold that as Pete walked, tool belt jangling, a cloud of white rose from his mouth. For a split second Finn wondered if Lilly was warm enough at the house. Then he remembered to call himself a fool for caring, because she wasn't at the house.

Dammit. How much longer until he forgot Lilly Churchill's existence? When would he forget the smell of her hair? Her breath? The sound of her laugh after they made love?

Time, man, he thought, giving himself a pep talk. *All I need is enough time and I'll forget about her just like I did Vivian.*

Heading for the thermos of coffee he kept in Abigail, he snorted.

If time was so all-fired important, then how come he'd gotten over Vivian's leaving in a day and here it was going on a month since he'd last seen Lilly and it still hurt to breathe? Everything hurt from his head to his heart to his soul. If the woman had been so hell-bent on destroying him, why hadn't she gone ahead and finished the job instead of leaving him in limbo like this?

He yanked open the passenger-side door of his truck and swore he caught a whiff of her perfume. He'd been doing that a lot lately and the habit was making him crazy.

Fumbling with unscrewing the cup and then the lid

to the thermos, he set them both on the edge of the seat and took a swig of lukewarm black coffee.

"Drinking straight from the bottle's hard core for this early in the morning, isn't it?" Matt strolled up behind him. The soles of his boots crunched on the frozen earth.

"Unless you have something work-related to say, with all respects, leave me the hell alone."

"No can do, bud." His best friend patted him on the back. The motion caused Finn to jerk away, in the process knocking the thermos lid off the seat and onto the truck's floorboard.

"Thanks a lot," Finn said, already bending to retrieve it, but Matt shot out his arm to stop him.

"Get that later. We need to talk."

"I already told you, I—"

"And I told you," Matt said, his voice uncharacteristically rough. "We need to talk and by God, if I have to move your lips myself, that's exactly what we're going to do."

"If this is about Lilly, I—"

"Your damned right it's about Lilly, but not how you think."

Finn hardened his jaw, furious at his friend for this invasion upon his private pain.

"Finn, man, you've gotta either get over her, which would be pretty stupid considering how much fun she was at poker night, or go get her—wherever the hell she went—but this black funk of yours can't go on. We lost three good men over at the motel site yesterday because they couldn't hack your temper."

"Yeah, well," Finn said, gazing out at the expansive view of rolling snow-covered foothills and the Wasatch Mountains beyond that. "If their egos were that fragile, we probably didn't need 'em anyway."

"Bull. They were good men, Finn. Men who have been with us for years. They were family men who appreciated the fact that you willingly gave them time off to take their kids to the dentist or go see a school play, but you're not that man anymore. Whatever happened with Lilly has changed you."

"I told you," Finn said, his teeth clenched, "I don't want to talk about her."

"If you don't want to talk about her, maybe you'll talk about this—that green tub you jumped Pete for mistakenly ordering?"

"Yeah?"

"While you were on your honeymoon, Mrs. Kleghorn wrote out a sixty-eight-hundred-dollar check for that monstrosity. She said some fool thing about it matching her favorite gemstone. Anyway, bottom line is that whether you like it or not, the tub is stayin'. Unlike Pete. He quit not three minutes after you called him an amateur."

Groaning, Finn put his hand to his forehead. "Crap. Go after him for me, would ya, Matt? Give him a five grand bonus and tell him I'm sorry."

"No can do," Matt said, standing his ground.

"Why the hell not?"

"Because if you've got an apology to make, the words should come from you. And while you're at it, I could use one, too."

Before Finn had a chance to say anything, Matt

stormed off, hopped in his red Chevy truck and aimed it toward the motel site.

Damn.

Finn hated losing a good plumber even worse than he'd hated losing a bad wife.

Leaning into the truck to fetch the fallen thermos lid, he hit his head on the door frame, which did nothing to soothe his already bearish mood. Cursing a blue streak, rubbing his head with one hand while reaching beneath the seat with the other, his fingers grasped not the plastic lid but cold glass. "What the…"

Eyebrows furrowed, at the same time he pulled the cylindrical object out, his heart broke anew.

It was a perfume bottle.

Or to be more precise, Lilly's perfume bottle. The fragrance was called Wildflower and he yanked off the lid, closed his eyes and held the bottle under his nose. The achingly familiar fragrance filled his eyes with tears.

Had she planted that bottle the night he'd left just to continuously torment him with her scent?

The practical side of him quickly squelched that irrational thought. He vaguely remembered her purse falling to the floorboard Thanksgiving morning. He'd been the one who'd abruptly pulled to the side of the road, so he was at fault for Abigail smelling more like his wife than his truck.

Could he be at fault for other things as well?

CHRISTMAS EVE, while the rest of the Churchill gang sat around the fire swapping holiday stories over cookies and cocoa, Lilly sat at the kitchen table, staring at the kitchen wall phone, willing it to ring.

Mary, a red Santa mug in hand, entered the room and sighed. "I thought you said you were going to the bathroom and then you'd be right back to the party?"

"I lied."

Pouring a fresh cup of cocoa, Mary said, "You've got to stop this moping, honey. If Finn is even half the man we all believe he is, he'll come around. But believe me," she said, and pulled out the chair beside Lilly's and sat down. "As an officially old married woman, I know firsthand how fragile a man's ego can be. Hearing the news about Elliot being the father of your baby didn't leave Finn much room to maneuver. He feels tricked, and only through time will he hopefully begin to see that wasn't the case."

"Yes, but what if he never sees me as anything but a conniving woman out to—as he so bluntly put it—find my baby and me a meal ticket? And *is* that what I was doing, Mary?"

Her sister took a sip of her steaming drink, taking her time to formulate an answer. "I guess maybe you were, little sis. And from what you told me about Dallas, he would have been using you to some extent to give himself an instant family to help his image at his law firm. The arrangement you'd made with him—while I deplore it—at least was based upon mutual understanding. For Finn, though, once he told you about his bet, he was never anything but straight with you. In return, he expected that same honesty."

Bowing her head, Lilly sighed. "I really messed up this time, didn't I?"

Mary set her mug on the table and pulled Lilly into a hug. "I'd be lying if I said you hadn't, but I'll make a deal with you." Pulling back, she brushed two tears from Lilly's cheeks.

"What?" she asked with a sniffle.

"If Finn hasn't come back to claim you by Valentine's Day, I'll drive you to Greenleaf myself and see what we can do about talking some sense into that man."

"*Valentine's Day?*" Lilly's eyes widened in horror. "I'll never survive that long without him."

"Oh, yes, you will. We Churchill women are strong." Tucking a fallen curl behind Lilly's ear, Mary said, "You've grown a lot in the past month. Mom and Dad just this morning told me how proud they are of you for owning up to your mistakes. We all think you deserve a second chance. In short, you've been very, very good." She winked. "Who knows, maybe tonight Santa will put Finn in your stocking?"

CHRISTMAS EVE, Finn sat on his favorite bar stool at Lu's, nursing a beer. The place was packed full of either partiers or loners like him who had no place else to go. Elvis crooned "Jingle Bell Rock" on the jukebox and Betty and Bob Bristow were dancing up a storm in matching red satin Santa suits.

Sighing, Finn tried his damnedest to block the noise and smelly cigar smoke, but it was no use. He'd come here to get his thoughts off Lilly, but the harder he tried forgetting her, the more she was on his mind.

The Elvis music took him back to that zany dog and bird show in Vegas and the way his wife had flashed him her adorable dimpled grin. The bar's smooth surface reminded him of the feel of her silky curls. Even the cigar smoke reminded him of her sexy slot playing.

"Can I get you a turkey dinner to go with your beer?" Lu asked.

"No, thanks. I don't much feel like eating."

"Come on, Finn, it's almost Christmas. Can't you give me even a puny smile?"

Only to please the woman who'd been like a second mother to him, he raised the corners of his mouth a fraction of an inch.

"Sorry to break this to you, son, but that wasn't a smile, but a frown."

"At least give me credit for trying. It's not my fault that my damned mouth doesn't work anymore."

"Judging by the foulness of your language, you're darned right it's not working and I'll bet I know the reason why."

"Hey, Lu!" Mitch called from the other end of the bar. "How about lettin' that loser rot in his own self-pity and gettin' me another beer?" He waved his empty mug.

"How about you shuttin' that hole in your face," she hollered back, "then gettin' off that big rear end of yours and fetchin' it yourself!"

Turning back to Finn, she said, "Where were we? Ah, yes, the reason why you've turned more crotchety than a two-legged dog tryin' to scratch a flea."

Finn rolled his eyes.

To which Lu promptly swatted him with her bar towel. "Don't you sass me, boy. You're still not too big for me to toss over my knee." Cracking a grin, she said, "Now, if the thought of little old me tryin' to wrestle you onto my lap didn't make you smile, I don't know what will."

"How about finding a woman who won't lie." He downed his last swig of beer.

"Funny, but I thought that was exactly what you'd found in that sweetheart, Lilly?"

"Are you kidding me? You know how she kept the real father of her baby from me, Lu. Even you can't deny that was a downright despicable thing to do."

"And you haulin' her off for a quickie Vegas wedding to save your truck wasn't?"

Eyes narrowed, he said, "You know what I'm talking about. She made a fool of me."

"No, the way I see it is, you're makin' a fool of you."

"I'm probably going to kick myself for asking, but how's that?"

"Because you've become a dawlgoned coward when it comes to love, Finn Reilly. Granted, what Vivian did to you was a cryin' shame, but Lilly is a far cry from Vivian. Since the first day you came in here, I've been hearin' these sob stories of how you want a wife and kids. Well, now you've finally got a beautiful, loving bride who every time she looks at you bursts into happy tears, and as if that weren't good enough, she comes complete with a baby on the way."

"Yeah," he said with a snort. "Some other guy's baby."

"If that's truly how you feel, then you're not half the man I thought you were. What? Just because that child's not yours, is that going to make him or her any less lovable? If anything, knowin' its real daddy would so shamelessly up and abandon his own flesh and blood and Lilly like he did should make you love that mother and child all the more.''

"If you're done scolding me," Finn said, waving his empty bottle, "may I please have another beer?"

Hands on her hips, she said, "No, you may not. And don't interrupt me when I'm on a roll. Just because your wife had a hard time tellin' you what was obviously a sensitive subject, are you honestly pigheaded enough to give up the dream you've spent your whole life tryin' to find?"

"What dream is that?"

"Ugh!" She threw her hands and the towel in the air. "I give up."

"Good."

"Good? That's it. Not only are you *not* gettin' another beer tonight, but either you come back with your bride in tow, or you're no longer welcome on these premises—ever."

"Aw, now, Lu, you don't mean that."

Jutting her chin as high as a barely five-foot-tall woman could, she said, "Try me."

Chapter Sixteen

At home, Finn fed his three mutts, made sure their heating lamp was on in the barn, then, since the small box by the road had been overflowing on his last drive by, he loped back across the snowy yard to grab the mail.

In the kitchen, he kicked off his work boots at the door, making sure not to look anywhere near the direction of the table, for if he did, he would see *her,* laughing over a plate of one of her delicious casseroles. But then if he looked toward the stove, he'd see her singing over a pot of spaghetti, and the memory of her angelic voice—not to mention the harmony she'd briefly brought to his home—would make his soul weep.

Unable to look anywhere but straight ahead without pain, he shuffled through the mail to find mostly sales circulars. A few bills and Christmas cards. He was about to set the pile on the counter before heading to bed when a small red envelope caught his attention. The return address read simply Vivian. The card had been postmarked in Galveston, Texas.

Frowning, he tossed the rest of the mail to the table before slipping his finger beneath the envelope's seal.

Hey Finn,

I guess sorry doesn't come close to making up for me running out on our wedding like I did, but with it being Christmas and all, I had to at least try explaining why I took off with Ray. Make no mistake, I did love you, and probably a part of me always will. But the way you put me on a pedestal, expecting me to be the perfect wife in that perfect house of yours, trying to be the living incarnation of all your dreams. It was just too hard. I knew I'd never live up to your standards, so I ran.

I'm doing fine. I found a job waitressing at a swanky place with a view of the beach, and Ray and I are still together. I'll always have a special place in my heart for you, Finn, and hope more than anything that one day you'll not only forgive me, but find that perfect woman you've been dreaming of—Vivian

Whew. By the time Finn finished reading, tears welled in his throat.

For all the reasons he'd imagined Vivian fleeing their wedding, never had he thought his high standards could be to blame. After all, what was wrong with a man expecting certain things from his wife? Namely, that she wouldn't ride off with a stranger on a motor-cycle at their wedding, or that she'd have the decency to tell him if she was pregnant with another man's child *before* they tied the knot.

Tossing Vivian's note onto the stack of mail already on the table, he stormed through the silent house, intent on building a fire. Since early that morning, cold had gripped him and wouldn't let go. But even when he had the fire crackling hot, Finn was still chilled to the bone. Only then did it dawn on him that the kind of warming he needed didn't come from outside, but inside.

Here it was Christmas Eve and he was all alone.

He had more friends than he could shake a stick at who'd invited him to share in their family festivities. Shoot, if he'd wanted, he could have walked the half mile down the road to Doc Walsh's, or for that matter, barged in on Randy and Chrissy's celebration, but he figured what was the point in celebrating when any glimmer of cheer he'd ever had was in a house over a hundred miles north?

Gazing out the darkened window, he wondered what Lilly was doing.

Singing around the fire with that wonderfully wacky family of hers? Had her mother made any of her caramel pecan rolls? For Christmas dinner would they be having turkey, ham or maybe even goose? And was Lilly showing yet? He'd always loved the sight of a pregnant woman. She'd be especially cute. If the baby was a girl, would she have her mom's thick head of curls? If it was a boy, would he have the straight Churchill blond hair Lilly's brothers had?

So many questions, he thought, washing his face

with his hands. But perhaps the biggest question of all was the one Lu had posed.

Just because your wife had a hard time tellin' you what was obviously a sensitive subject, are you honestly pigheaded enough to give up the dream you spent your whole life tryin' to find?

Was he that pigheaded?

In the days he'd been away from Lilly, he'd gone over their time together with a fine-tooth comb. He searched his memory for ways she'd deliberately tried deceiving him, but no matter how hard he tried, he found none. In fact, if he were totally truthful, he remembered times she must have tried to tell him about the baby, but for different reasons, he'd cut her off.

Like the ghost of Christmas past, Vivian's words haunted him, too.

…you put me on a pedestal, expecting me to be the perfect wife in that perfect house of yours, trying to be the living incarnation of all your dreams. It was just too hard. I knew I'd never live up to your standards, so I ran.

Could Vivian be right? Had he held not only her, but Lilly to impossible standards? Could Lilly have been telling the truth when she'd told him repeatedly Thanksgiving night that she'd wanted to tell him about her baby but had been too afraid?

In the hall, the grandfather clock struck twelve.

Christmas Day. The ultimate day for forgiveness and new beginnings.

Looking back on all the kids he'd loved over the course of his life, he remembered countless Cub Scout troops, Randy and Chrissy, baby Abby. None of those children had been his, yet that technicality hadn't made him love them any less.

So why should it be any different with Lilly's baby?

A baby who, if Finn would only open his heart, would love him like a daddy—or maybe even more.

And Lilly. As much as he'd told himself Vivian had ruined him for life in the love department, he'd been wrong. He did love Lilly. He loved her more than he'd thought it was possible to love, which was why it hurt so damned much having her gone. But it didn't have to be that way. Yes, during the course of their whirlwind relationship, they'd both made huge mistakes, but what if they wiped the slate clean? What if starting right now, on Christmas Day, they started over? All their secrets out in the open. All their love ready and willing to give.

Anticipation filling his soul, he raced up the stairs.

In the back of his top dresser drawer, he kept his mother's jewelry box. If he was going to do this thing, he might as well do it right, starting by proposing to Lilly this time as Finn—not Dallas. And in order to do that, he needed a piece of his past to form a shining bridge to his future.

By God, Lilly might have entered his life via blind luck, but if he had anything to do with it, she'd be staying in his life via determination!

Boom.

Boom boom.

Lilly, fitfully sleeping, thought she must have dreamed the odd sound, but sure enough, there it was again, a solid thumping against her window. Slipping out from under her floral down comforter, she went to the window to have a look.

Finn? Throwing snowballs?

Now she knew she was dreaming. She was heading back to bed when a voice stopped her.

"Lilly!" he shouted. "I'm sorry! Meet me at the front door!"

Heart pounding, she didn't bother slipping on a robe or slippers over Finn's Greenleaf High T-shirt and thick white socks. All she knew was that the sooner she got to the front door, the sooner she'd know whether or not she was still asleep.

Racing down the stairs, turning the lock, then yanking open the big front door, at first, all she saw was swirling snow, but then he was there, brushing past her to enter the front hall.

"Hi," he said, blowing on his bare hands. "It's cold."

"It usually is on Christmas."

He grinned. "You look gorgeous, and I'm glad to see my foolishness hasn't caused you to change your taste in fashion."

Though she wasn't sure whether to laugh or cry, she said, "What are you doing here? It's got to be one or two in the morning."

"Actually, it's almost three, but I figured, what the heck? I might as well get a head start on my holiday gift giving."

"Is—is that why you're here?" she said, tucking flyaway curls behind her ears. "Because you want to give someone a gift?"

"Not just someone, Lilly...*you.*"

"Santa?" said a sleepy child from the living room. "Is that you?"

"Go back to sleep, Erin," Lilly said to her niece. To Finn she said, "All the kids are bedded down in the living room and den. Why don't we talk in the kitchen?"

"Sure. Lead the way."

She did, feeling self-conscious about the length—or rather lack of length—of her borrowed T-shirt. Why was he here? Was he coming to make up? Was he willing to accept Elliot's baby as his own? Could she really be so lucky?

In the kitchen, she flicked on the light over the sink, then asked, "Can I get you anything? Cocoa? Tea?" *Me?* He looked even more handsome than she remembered, his dark hair all mussed and made darker by melting snow. He wore faded jeans and a hip-length brown leather jacket that did heavenly things to his eyes.

"Thanks," he said, "but all I really need is for you to sit down."

"O-okay." She did as he asked, pulling out a chair at the table, trying to tug her T-shirt lower on her way down.

"You must be cold," he said, shrugging off his coat and placing it over her bare legs. It smelled of leather and him, and still radiated with his warmth.

"Mmm, that feels good," she said. *Almost as good as once again being with you.*

"I'm glad, you know, that you're warm." Turning his back to her, he rubbed his face with his hands before spinning back around. "On the ride up here, I had all this worked out, but now I'm not sure where to begin.''

"How about if I start?" Lilly said, her voice quiet in the cold, still night. From upstairs, she heard a floorboard squeak and in the kitchen, she jumped when the refrigerator motor clicked on. "Look at me," she said with a nervous giggle. "I'm even more jittery now than when you left."

"I'm sorry about the way I took off like that. You were right, we should have talked."

"No, I was wrong. We should have talked all right, but back in Vegas when you first told me you weren't Dallas. I'm so sorry, Finn, I never meant to hurt you that way. I…" She wrung her hands. "Once I realized how much I loved you, I was afraid if I told you the truth about Elliot being my baby's father you'd stop loving me."

"Never," he said, crossing the short distance to her and kneeling on the hardwood floor to draw her into his arms.

"But you did stop loving me, Finn. Exactly what I was afraid of happening happened."

"Because I'm a fool."

"No, don't call yourself that. I understand why you were upset."

"But being upset didn't give me the right to run out on you like I did."

"Okay," she said with a nervous laugh, "we've both made mistakes, but what should we do about them?"

Reaching into his front pocket, he withdrew a black velvet ring box. "I don't know about you, but this is what I want to do.'' Popping open the box, he took out a ruby and diamond ring. Holding it between his trembling thumb and forefinger, he said, ''This was both my grandmother's and mother's engagement ring. I wanted to give it to you on our wedding day in Vegas, but, well, you know how that turned out. Anyway, I'm giving it to you now in the hopes that you'll forgive me, then marry me all over again. This time, with your dad walking you down the aisle and your mom baking us a great cake, your sisters acting as bridesmaids and hopefully, I can borrow a few of your brothers to stand beside Matt as my grooms.''

Lilly was sobbing so hard with a mixture of joy and relief that she couldn't even speak.

''Angel? I know the baby makes you overly emotional and stuff, but I'm dying here. Is that a yes or no?''

She sobbed all the harder.

''I, ah, know our first marriage was built on a weak foundation, but I am a contractor, sweetheart. I specialize in renovations. If you'll give me a yes, I promise to spend the rest of my life building the perfect marriage for us both.''

''Oh, F-Finn,'' she said. ''I love you....''

''Then that's a yes?''

''O-of c-course it's a yes.''

''Okay then, whew.'' Finn felt dizzy with relief. He'd come so close to throwing this wondrous relationship away, that now that he'd officially saved it, he felt like joining in on Lilly's latest batch of tears. ''I guess that settles it. We're going to have a wedding and a baby.''

"Does that mean we can all join in on the celebration?" Mary asked from the kitchen door.

"How long have you been standing there?" Lilly asked.

"Long enough," she said, running across the room to crush her sister, then brother-in-law in a hug. "Congratulations. When Erin came and told me Santa wasn't here, but Uncle Finn was, I took the liberty of waking the rest of the troop."

One by one, the rest of Lilly's pajama-clad, sleepy but happy family filed past, shaking Finn's hand and patting him on the back.

On the ride up, he'd feared them holding a grudge, but nothing could have been further from the truth. They all shared stories of times during their marriages that they'd been through rough patches and expressed their joy that he and Lilly had survived theirs.

Around five-thirty, Lilly's mom took fresh caramel pecan rolls from the oven before passing around a fragrant pot of coffee. From his seat across the room from his wife, Finn caught Lilly's gaze and held it.

Crooking his finger, while the rest of her family happily chattered around them, he beckoned her to him. When she perched on his lap, it took his body less than half a second to recall other times she'd been this close, and how nearly every single one of those times had turned out.

"Merry Christmas," he whispered in her ear.

"Merry Christmas," she whispered back.

"Think anyone would notice if we slipped away for our own private celebration?"

Seeing that her brothers were engrossed in the prospect of the Utah Jazz having a winning season and her sisters and mom were planning her second wedding, she shook her head. "Nope, looks like the coast is clear."

Finn gave her a swift but passionate kiss, then scooped her into his arms.

They were about to make a clean getaway when Mary called out, "Sleep tight, you two!"

"We will," Lilly said with a wave.

"The hell we will," Finn said in the privacy of the hall, giving her one more kiss before mounting the stairs.

His mind spinning with joy and relief and even sadness for the time they'd lost, Finn couldn't help but remember how long he'd dreamed of this very moment. Best of all, it hadn't taken a bet to find true love…just blind luck.

Epilogue

A year later, Christmas night, after the gifts had been opened, the turkey eaten and the good china put away, Lilly drew her husband into the laundry room. Granted, with both the washer and dryer chugging, it wasn't the most romantic spot to give him one more gift, but considering how many people filled her parents' house, it was the most private.

"Mmm," he said from his perch against the dryer. "Now that Charlotte's finally asleep, you're stealing me away for a little hanky-panky, are you, Mrs. Claus?"

"Brilliant deductive reasoning, Mr. Claus." She lightly jingled his Santa hat's bell. "But in this case you're wrong."

"Oh?" Hands on her hips, he cinched her close, slanting his lips atop hers for a mind-blowing kiss. When he succeeded in turning her mind to needful mush, he pulled back. "Well, Mrs. Claus? Wasn't there something you needed to be doing other than ravaging your poor, helpless husband?"

"Yeah," she said with a grin. "Bonking you on your big head with that giant candy cane you gave the baby—like she can really eat something that big, Finn.''

"Hey, she's got teeth."

"Two!"

"Tell me," he said, stealing a quick nibble on her ear. "Have I committed any other fathering sins? Have I scalded her with too hot bathwater? Poked her in the eye with a rogue *bumblebee, bumblebee* spoon?"

"No."

"Okay. And how many times have you had her over to Doc Walsh's for ridiculous reasons?"

"Hey," she said, giving Santa a poke in his belly. "She said it was perfectly normal for me to be concerned about Charlotte's early penchant for Minnie Mouse shaped ice cream sandwiches. What if she chokes on a stick?"

"Never happen. Remember? I hold on to the sticks."

"One might gag her."

"Nope."

"Stab her?"

He sighed. "Give it up, sweetie. Let's face it, I am the perfect dad."

Even in teasing, Lilly couldn't find fault with that statement, so standing on her tiptoes, she gave him another lingering kiss.

"Wow. What did I do to deserve that?"

"You're you. I love you, you know."

"I love you, too. We have a great life, you, me and Charlotte."

Too choked up to speak, she nodded.

"What's wrong? You look close to spouting one of those gushers you used to when you were pregnant."

"Uh-huh. It's just that I'm so h-happy. It's Christmas and we're here with all our family, and I'm finally pregnant again with—" Tears really flowing, she flew her hand to her mouth. "No, no, no. I can't believe I spilled my own secret. The new baby was supposed to be a surprise. I have gift-wrapped booties stashed in the washer and everything."

"Sweetie, I hate to be the bearer of bad news, but sounds like the washer just kicked into the spin cycle."

"Oh no!" Lunging for the lid, she raised it, but by the time the barrel stopped spinning, it was too late. Her prettily wrapped package with its pink and blue ribbon was ruined. "Why does this kind of thing always h-happen to me?" she sobbed against her husband's chest. "Why am I constantly messing things up?"

Far from being upset by the incident, Finn worked hard to hold back a laugh, but didn't quite succeed. "Can you believe it? I'm going to be a father— again!"

"This isn't funny. I wanted this announcement to be a special moment for you."

"Baby—or I guess that would be, *Mommy*," he said, his mouth frozen in what he feared would be a nine-month-long grin, "You've just given me the happiest news of my life and you think a pair of wet booties is going to ruin it?"

She shook her head and dried her eyes on the tails of his red flannel shirt.

"Look at me," he urged, softly nudging her pouting chin upward. "Haven't you figured it out yet?"

"What?"

"I love you. I love the way you turn all my white T-shirts pink. I love the way the slightest peep out of Charlotte sends you into a tizzy. Hell, I even love the way you've somehow fertilized-to-death over ninety percent of my ferns."

"I have not!"

"Have, too," he said, drawing her into yet another fervent kiss. "Mmm, and I especially love your way with—"

"Knock, knock." Mary stood at the laundry room door, a cooing, wide-eyed Charlotte in her arms. "Sorry to interrupt this late-night smooch-a-thon, but I caught this kiddo trying to escape her crib." She eyed Finn. "*Someone* must've sneaked her too much candy and now she's ready for action."

"Give me Daddy's girl," Finn said, his heart so full of love for his wife and daughter and the new addition to their family on his or her way, he felt ready to burst. Mary handed him the baby, and with the munchkin already cooing, he bounced her a few times to really get her juices flowing. "No kid can ever have too much candy on Christmas, can they, my little pumpkin pie?"

Hands cupping her tummy, Lilly cast her daughter and husband an indulgent grin. As usual, Finn was right, but far from being upset by the fact, it only made her love him—and their life—more.

Never had she felt happier. More complete. It was as if up until finding him, a piece of herself had been missing. But now, Finn's love shone in her heart like a beacon, lighting the way to his loving arms, finally making her see that while she might always be a misfit, as long as she had Finn for a husband, best friend and lover, she was the luckiest misfit in the world.

Say "I do" with

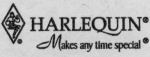

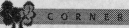

COOPER'S CORNER

The latest continuity from Harlequin Books continues in October 2002 with

STRANGERS WHEN WE MEET
by Marisa Carroll

Check-in: Radio talk-show host Emma Hart thought Twin Oaks was supposed to be a friendly inn, but fellow guest Blake Weston sure was grumpy!

Checkout: When both Emma and Blake find their fiancés cheating on them, they find themselves turning to one another for support—and comforting hugs quickly turn to passionate embraces....

HARLEQUIN®
Makes any time special®

Visit us at www.cooperscorner.com

CC-CNM3

ƑALL IN ℒOVE
THIS WINTER
WITH
HARLEQUIN BOOKS!

In October 2002 look for these special volumes
led by *USA TODAY* bestselling authors,
and receive a MOULIN ROUGE VHS video*!
*Retail value of $14.99 U.S.

See inside books for details.

**This exciting promotion
is available at your
favorite retail outlet.**

Only from

HARLEQUIN®

Makes any time special ®

Visit Harlequin at www.eHarlequin.com   PHNCP02

If you enjoyed what you just read,
then we've got an offer you can't resist!

Take 2 bestselling love stories FREE!
Plus get a FREE surprise gift!

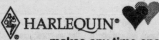

Princes...Princesses...
London Castles...New York Mansions...
To live the life of a royal!

**In 2002, Harlequin Books lets you escape to a
world of royalty with these royally themed titles:**

Temptation:
January 2002—*A Prince of a Guy* (#861)
February 2002—*A Noble Pursuit* (#865)

American Romance:
The Carradignes: American Royalty (Editorially linked series)
March 2002—*The Improperly Pregnant Princess* (#913)
April 2002—*The Unlawfully Wedded Princess* (#917)
May 2002—*The Simply Scandalous Princess* (#921)
November 2002—*The Inconveniently Engaged Prince* (#945)

Intrigue:
The Carradignes: A Royal Mystery (Editorially linked series)
June 2002—*The Duke's Covert Mission* (#666)

Chicago Confidential
September 2002—*Prince Under Cover* (#678)

The Crown Affair
October 2002—*Royal Target* (#682)
November 2002—*Royal Ransom* (#686)
December 2002—*Royal Pursuit* (#690)

Harlequin Romance:
June 2002—*His Majesty's Marriage* (#3703)
July 2002—*The Prince's Proposal* (#3709)

Harlequin Presents:
August 2002—*Society Weddings* (#2268)
September 2002—*The Prince's Pleasure* (#2274)

Duets:
September 2002—*Once Upon a Tiara/Henry Ever After* (#83)
October 2002—*Natalia's Story/Andrea's Story* (#85)

**Celebrate a year of royalty with
Harlequin Books!**

Available at your favorite retail outlet.

HARLEQUIN®
Makes any time special ®

Visit us at www.eHarlequin.com

HSROY02

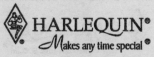